Terminal Hitman

Jeff Bonilla

Customer Reviews

“We all love justifiable and well-planned revenge. Interest is held throughout, cleverly using situations and emotions we all know well. A memorable tale with a perfect ending.”

“AMAZING BOOK! An exciting revenge thriller with a touch of dark humor. If you like books that read like a movie, with 5 page chapters and fast, exciting plots, clever twists, and plenty of laugh-out-loud moments, this book is for you. If you were ever bullied in grade school, and dreamt of getting even, this book is for you. If you prefer complex, human heroes and villains with a mixture of light and dark traits to the one-dimensional variety that Hollywood usually serves up, this book is for you. Can't recommend it highly enough.”

“As someone who was bullied in High school, I reveled with delight in each revenge kill Lol! Although the main character would be considered an anti-hero, I still found myself rooting for him…clearly LOL. Enjoy!!”

“"Terminal Hitman," by Jeff Bonilla, is a real treat. It has the right mix of humor, violence and suspense to make it a very enjoyable read. The plot and the characters are well-written and I was hooked on the novel right from the start. We figure out what is going to happen (we think), early in the novel, and I expected there to be a lack of suspense because of that. But that simply wasn't true. I was eager to find out HOW the plot would play out and also was pleasantly surprised by some twists in the story that I didn't see coming. Tom Hitsman, the protagonist, is a sympathetic character that I rooted for, despite some of his actions that could best be described as off-kilter. Also, if you like pop music like I do, you'll enjoy the various musical references, and it is a joy to discover the role Barry Manilow(!) plays in one of the killings. "Terminal Hitman" is a well-written and very enjoyable book. I would highly recommend this entertaining novel!”

Library of Congress Cataloging-in-Publication Data has been applied for.

ISBN: 13 - 979-8546407889

Cover Design: SelfPubBookCovers.com/DawnyDawny

Dedication

For the children in the darkness awaiting the light.

Acknowledgments

To all who stand up to tyranny and corruption and still believe in Truth, Justice and the American Way.

Contents

Darkness

Paul Clark blinked a few times as he regained consciousness. Groggy, his head felt like water sloshing around in a fishbowl. There was a bright spotlight aimed at him, burning his retinas. He was sitting in a chair, he finally deduced as he tried to get up, but couldn't. *Strange*, he thought.

Paul tried moving again, but nothing worked. He thought he was paralyzed but then felt restraints around his wrists locking his arms to the back of the chair; his feet also bound to the front legs of the chair. Chilled to the bone from fright, but also because he was naked, it was at this moment Paul realized he was in a precarious position. Darkness surrounded him except for the harsh spotlight. Senses slowly coming back, he felt a bulky object in his mouth preventing him from speaking or screaming for help.

A few hours ago, he had filled his last prescription at the pharmacy and headed to his car, a new gunmetal grey Mazda 6. His fun car. He was going to stop on the way home and buy some pizza for the wife and kids. Pizza Rev was his favorite pizza joint. Now, he was God knows where tied up like some kind of informant that was about to get capped. But how did this happen?

"I guess you're wondering how this happened?" said a voice from somewhere in the darkness. A silhouette shape moved in front of the spotlight and stepped close. "Long time no see, Paul." Although the shape was two feet closer, Paul could still not make out the man's facial features as he was lit from behind and shrouded in shadows. Yet, something stirred in the deep recesses of his memory. The voice... He had heard it before. A long, long, time ago.

"It's been a long time. Shit, over thirty years. I still can't believe I'll soon qualify for the senior discount at Denny's. How crazy is that, Paul?" Paul's muffled voice and wide eyes made the man chuckle. "I'm glad you could make this private reunion. Just you and me. Your buddy Kent Lim won't be screeching up in his Mustang to rescue you this time. You remember that, don't you? Riding shotgun in his brand new Mustang that his rich dad bought him when he turned sixteen. Spoiled brat, that Kent. And he didn't care about shoving it in everyone's face. He decided that you would be Chewy to his Han Solo, and you jumped at the chance. You and I had been friends since grammar school, but you broke off our friendship because of him. Just because he had money…. You made high school a very lonely place for me, Paul."

Beads of sweat sprouted like cornfields across Paul's forehead as he tried to speak but was unable to due to the object lodged in his mouth.

Laughing, the man said, "Sorry, Paul, but I can't understand a word you're saying. But that is fine. I'm not interested in what you have to say. What I am interested in is this." The man reached down between Paul's legs and lifted a tubular object that had been resting between his feet, holding it up for Paul to see. "Well, what do we have here? Looks like a fire extinguisher you might find in your kitchen."

Paul's moist forehead furled.

"Hmm, is that a look of total recall or a 'what the fuck' look?" Paul shook his head left to right. "I'm disappointed. I hoped this would have brought back some memories for you. It does for me."

Drenched in sweat, his mind racing, Paul strained his wrists against the flex cuffs that were keeping him bound to the chair. He was trapped.

"You know what this makes me think of? My old Dodge Colt. My first car. Yeah, it wasn't the sexiest of cars, kind of grandfatherish truth be told, and not cool like Kent's Mustang, but it was my first car. And you know your first car in high school is always a big deal. Like your first girl. You'll always remember her. They are both rites of passage from boyhood to manhood. But you know you couldn't even let me enjoy that. The morning after I bought it, I ran out to drive it to school for the first time. Man, I was so excited to take her out for a spin, but when I got to the driveway, I couldn't believe my eyes. My car was covered in some kind of grey powder. One of the windows was broken and the entire inside of the car was smeared with that same powder. How do you think that made me feel, Paul?"

A soft sob escaped from Paul as tears trickled down his face.

"No, Paul, I didn't cry.... But you're right, there was a sense of sadness. My best friend had not only turned his back on me but was going out of his way to fuck with me. It's heartbreaking when I reflect on it now. Well, we both know what the powder turned out to be, don't we?"

The man held up the fire extinguisher closer to Paul's face. That's when Paul saw that the nozzle from the extinguisher was running into his mouth. It was tightly sealed with black duct tape. That's why he couldn't talk. Paul's eyes flew open wide as he screamed and squirmed to no avail.

"That's right, Paul, you emptied a fire extinguisher into my car. I'll give it to you, it was a step above TP'ing a house.

A really good prank. Well, I hope that prank you pulled was worth it and that you and Kent laughed the hardest you have ever laughed in your entire life because that prank will now cost you your life."

Paul's eyes pleaded with the man.

"Yeah, I know, this is kind of fucked up, right? I mean, you were just a teenager doing teenager shit. Now you're a family man with a wife and kids and a house in the suburbs. You're getting ready to retire and enjoy your golden years. You're living the American dream—well, except for this part. This is what you call a twist in the story, a fly in the ointment."

Paul sobbed, heaving and having trouble catching his breath. The man held up the fire extinguisher to have a closer look.

"Let's see what the instructions say. You must be eight feet away. Well, not gonna be able to follow that instruction. What else... Do not ingest. Oops. Yeah, definitely not following that one." The man looked at the instructions and then shrugged. "I guess we'll just have to improvise."

Paul was whimpering as he tried rocking from side to side in a last-ditch effort to break free. The man put two gloved fingers under Paul's chin and lifted his head up so he could make eye contact with him.

"If it's any consolation, Kent will be joining you soon. Oh yeah, I didn't tell you? I've got plans for him. Trust me when I tell you, you're getting off easy compared to what I have prepared for him. Oh, you're not going to warn him, are you?" The man howled with laughter. "Wow! I'm really enjoying this. DAMN! What a fucking high! If I had known getting high felt this good, I would have done drugs with the rest of you assholes back in high school."

The man's laughter echoed in the dark, empty space. Then, just as suddenly, he stopped, took a long deep breath, looked skyward, and closed his eyes as if in contemplation.

"Ok, let's not lose focus here. Let's get back to you. Right now, it's all about you, Paul. First off, I'm sure this will taste like shit. Second, I'm going to empty the entire canister into your mouth, so you'll just have to get used to it. My guess is that you'll suffocate or the force will blast the back of your head off. I really don't know, I've never done this before. So…you ready?"

Paul's throat was raw from screaming and groaning, his muscles burned from straining to get loose. He would have cut both his hands off to escape this nightmare. His pleading tear-filled eyes looked up at the man, his childhood friend.

"Ok, let's rock and roll. Oh wait, I almost forgot." The man aimed a little remote control off to the side, and suddenly the opening guitar riffs to AC/DC's "Highway to Hell" exploded from a boombox somewhere in the darkness. "Thought you'd enjoy this blast from the past since it was one of Kent's favorite tunes to crank up while cruising with that cheese-rat grin of his."

Paul pissed himself as the man got a breath away from his sweaty face.

"Goodbye, Paul. This has been by far the best high school reunion ever."

Paul moaned at the top of his voice as the man pulled the pin from the fire extinguisher and squeezed the handle.

Zero Day Exploits

Three Months Earlier.

FastTrek Industries - Marina Del Rey, California

Tom Hitsman shook hands with CEO Arthur Levits and CTO Charles Grimes and took a seat across from them in the small utilitarian conference room. There was a big screen TV on the wall and a remote camera for conferencing, which he had done a few days earlier prior to the in-person meeting. Tom still couldn't get used to the idea that nowadays kids half his age were running multi-million-dollar companies. He certainly wasn't running a million-dollar company when he was in his twenties. Lucky for him, he still looked younger than his age and was still in good shape—of which he could only give thanks to his genes, being that he spent most of his time at a computer terminal and wasn't always diligent with his workout routines.

"Thanks for making the drive out," said Arthur with a cheery smile. "Hopefully you didn't hit too much traffic."

"No, I did ok. I just turn on a Kindle Audible book on long drives. It helps pass the time, and I'm less inclined to want to kill some fool for cutting me off," Tom replied with a knowing smirk.

"Exactly," Arthur replied. "You come highly recommended. As you know, we are getting ready to roll out our new software applications and we can't afford to have any breaches. Charles said you hacked into our system with no problem, and he still can't figure out how you did it."

"It's what I do."

"Well, you got my attention, because creating an impenetrable system is what I do, and yet you got in. How did you do it?" asked the chief technology officer, Charles Grimes.

Tom looked at both millennials and checked his body language against theirs. They were pretty relaxed, so he leaned back and went into his pitch. "Despite arguments to the contrary by Microsoft and other software companies, the truth is, it just isn't possible to create a flawless software program. In this day and age of information warfare, hackers everywhere from Silicon Valley to China to Russia probe companies looking for vulnerabilities or a single point of failure that they can exploit and act upon immediately. It's known as Zero Day Exploits. If I had been a hacker, your data library with all your customers' information would be on the dark web right now being sold to the highest bidder. Any proprietary technological information would also be compromised. Or, worse, you'd be at the mercy of ransomware. Geeks rule the world now." Tom looked at the young chief technology officer and said, "No offense intended."

"None taken," responded Charles.

"That's a scary scenario," said Arthur.

"Can you fix it or show my team how to fix it?" countered Charles.

"Yes, it's fixable. I can meet your deadline, but we would have to start sooner rather than later."

"Fantastic. Let's do this," said an enthusiastic Arthur as he pushed back from his chair.

"Well, that was easy," replied Tom.

"I don't mess around. We'll get the contract signed and back to you. C'mon, I'll walk you out."

The three men exited the glass-encased conference room and walked down the hallway. Tom marveled not only at the fancy tech-inspired art that lined the hallway walls, but at the young employees who all seemed to be under thirty years of age. Had everyone been under thirty when he first entered the job market? No, he remembered a lot of older men in the workforce when he first started. *Now he was the old man*, he thought to himself as he caught his reflection off one of the glass conference rooms. *Man, where did the time go?* At least he still had his health and a certain degree of coolness without trying too hard. No growing a ponytail or piercing his left ear as Harrison Ford had done to hold on to some degree of coolness, though.

Didn't Harrison realize he was coolness defined and didn't need any additional accouterments to reinforce...the force? *Ok, lame joke*, he thought to himself, but it made him smile. Two young female employees reciprocated his smile as he walked past them. One of them reminded him of Amy, the girl he was currently involved with. On second thought, entangled might have been a better word. He remembered they had a dinner date later that night at his place and wondered what fantasy she was going to play out tonight. As Arthur babbled on about his company, Tom suddenly felt a sharp pain reverberate through his abdomen. It was fleeting but it caught his attention. *That was odd*, he thought. Before he could give it more thought, Arthur stuck out his hand and Tom realized they were back at the lobby. They shook hands and exchanged pleasantries, and Tom stepped out into a beautiful Southern California day. How lucky he was to be alive and doing what he loved to do and living in the best place in the world. No earring required.

The Neighbor

The drive back from Orange County to Ventura County had taken much too long. Tom walked into his luxury condo and was greeted at the door by his best buddy Marty, a Lhasa Apso-Maltese mix. Marty spun in circles, which was his customary greeting and show of affection for Tom. Four years ago, Tom had been in a bad part of town and saw the dog hopping away from some kids who were chasing it. All too familiar with being bullied, he pulled his car over and glared at the teens who stopped in their tracks and backed off.

He took the dog to a vet and paid for the treatment. A few days later, the veterinarian called him and said no one had claimed the dog. Tom picked him up and took him home. The dog was hobbling around in a cast but seemed to be happy he was somewhere safe. They watched *Back to the Future* that night, and that's when the dog got the name Marty, as in Marty Mcfly.

"Hey, buddy, you hungry?" Marty knew what that meant and spun in a tight circle.

Tom finished feeding Marty and then flipped on the TV and went through his mail, separating the envelopes into neat stacks: "Trash" and "Read" stacks. One envelope caught his eye, and he slipped it out and opened it up. It was from his high school. It never ceased to amaze him how they could track you down—especially when they needed donations.

As he skimmed the letter, his eyes darted to the bold, fancy headline, *Class of 1989 30th Reunion.* High school had not been a fun place for him, and he hadn't gone back to any of his previous reunions. He continued to read the invitation and saw that they were going to be having the dedication ceremony to the newly refurbished auditorium and new gym courtesy of Kent Lim: the Kent Lim Gym. How apropos. Now he was sure he wouldn't be going back to the reunion. After all this time he still had a burning hatred for Kent.

Kent came from a rich Korean family and had no problem flaunting his privileged wealth in front of everyone. He was a constant eyesore, speeding up and down the streets, around the school grounds, and burning rubber in the parking lot with his new Mustang Cobra 2. His two sidekicks Paul Clark and Darren Gilman were permanent fixtures in his car. The senior yearbook had voted them most likely to die in a fiery car crash. When the faculty decided to put speed bumps in the student parking lot, Kent was the first one out there pouring gasoline on the speed bumps and spinning his tires on top of them, thereby doing his best to disintegrate them. He was also the supplier of porn magazines and alcohol to the freshman class. All and all, he was a real spoiled brat, but that wasn't what bothered Tom. Paul Clark and Tom had been good friends since grammar school, but Kent had recruited Paul as his bestie, and they had both gone out of their way to make senior year miserable for Tom. Kids could be so cruel.

Suddenly there was a rat-tat-tat on the door which knocked Tom out of his reverie. He recognized it as his neighbor's knock—Randy Montrose. As is the case in many complexes, there's always a neighbor that is troublesome in one way or another, and the luxury condos Tom resided in were no exception to this rule. He muted the TV and got up to let Randy in, knowing that in fifteen minutes he would come up with some excuse to dispatch him. Fifteen minutes was about all he could tolerate. *Small doses*, he thought to himself.

Randy came flying in through the door in a rage and stormed into the living room. "Can you believe this!? Some bitch is pulling the #MeToo bullshit on me and suing me!"

"You're getting sued for sexual harassment?"

"No! She's claiming I gave her autism!" countered Randy.

"What?"

Randy scanned pages from a document he was holding. "She's claiming that because I slipped off my condom while in the middle of having intercourse with her, that I violated her physically and emotionally and put her at risk of contracting a sexually transmitted disease or even a life-threatening disease like AIDS." Randy flipped to the next page. "The suit claims that since the incident she has been suffering from memory loss, a loss of certain basic motor skills such as speech control, and impairment of social interaction and communication. Therefore, she claims my assault on her has triggered late-onset autism!"

Thinking it was a prank, Tom laughed. "You're joking, right?"

"Oh, and she has had a burning sensation ever since I spilled my baby batter. This is going to cost me money and ruin my reputation." Randy threw a thick document down onto the coffee table.

Tom reached for the documents. "Let me see this." He picked up the documents and perused them, flipping through the pages. After a few moments, he frowned and put them back down. "Wow. You weren't kidding. I've never seen anything like this. I didn't even know you could sue someone for giving them autism." Tom chuckled.

"I'm glad you find it humorous! The worst part is she is posting this shit all over social media with a link to my picture!"

"Really? Let's have a look."

Tom sat at his computer, and for the next half hour, they reviewed all her social media accounts. Her name was Nina Cobra—a stage name as she was a wannabe model/actress/stripper. She was a brunette with a hard body, full lips, and crazy eyes. She claimed to be twenty-seven, but she looked more like a well-preserved thirty-seven. Her resume had various modeling assignments for men's magazines, such as *Easy Rider*, *Born to Ride*, and *Legs International*. She also had some credits on what appeared to be porn movies and a scat clip.

"Jesus, Randy. You should be suing her! God knows what you might have picked up from her. And why on earth would you take off your condom with a crazy chick like this?"

"I hate condoms," Randy sheepishly responded.

Tom noticed the Batman t-shirt Randy was wearing. "You need the bat helmet if you're going into the Batcave, you know what I mean?"

As they continued to review her Facebook account they saw derogatory remarks about Randy, but also saw all kinds of crazy rantings and racial slanders about other actors and agents and society in general. There were nonsensical sentences that seemed to indicate she might be suffering from some kind of mental illness or even a split personality.

"Well, my friend, you picked a winner. In keeping with the theme here, I think she is bat-shit crazy. Just print out her rantings on Facebook and take them to court. Any judge worth his gavel will throw this out."

"Yeah, but I don't want everyone knowing I did her." Randy looked at Tom with sad puppy dog eyes. "Can't you do something?"

"What do you mean?"

"C'mon, man. I'm not an idiot. No one has this kind of setup unless they are into some real heavy online, dark web kinda stuff." Randy nodded to Tom's computer. "A custom-built liquid cooled computer and five terabyte external hard drives. I know about that kind of setup, and I know you can help me out."

Tom contemplated it for a moment. "How did you meet her?"

"I did some graphic design for a couple of guys who shoot porn out in Canoga Park. They invited me down to one of their shoots. She was one of their girls. She was probably off her meds the day I met her cause normally I wouldn't have had a shot with someone as hot as her."

Tom looked at Randy. He was in his late twenties, height-challenged, acne-pocked skin, doughy body with jet black hair scooped in a Ritchie Valens pompadour. He was probably right. Under normal circumstances, he probably wouldn't have had a chance. He was a classic man-child. If there was one redeeming quality, it was that Randy was an audiophile. Tom could appreciate that quality.

"Out of curiosity, how was she?"

Randy's face lit up as he recalled the memory. "She was like a Kansas tornado. Made my head spin. At one point I thought I saw Toto flying past my bed."

Tom rubbed his chin and then grinned. "Yeah, I'll help you out."

"Seriously!?" exclaimed Randy.

"Yeah."

Randy pumped his fist in the air. "Ah man, that's great. What about the court document?"

"I'll take care of it."

"And her social media?" asked Randy.

"Buh bye Facebook."

"Yes! You da man! Thank you. I owe you one." Randy got up and headed for the door with a bounce in his step. "I gotta do some work for another porn client, but if you need anything just let me know."

Randy let himself out, which was a first, and Tom started typing, his fingers flying on the keyboard. He had never hacked into the Los Angeles County Courthouse system before, but he wasn't too concerned. That was child's play for someone with his skill set.

Amy

Amy and Tom finished washing the dishes and then sat down on the expansive red leather couch to watch TV. They liked watching cop shows and true-life crime dramas. He was pretty sure that if he ever needed to pull off a crime, he could probably get away with it. Most criminals were morons and most cops were lazy. At least in his opinion. All someone needed was half a brain and an imaginative stratagem that was meticulously planned out and they could be successful. Tom was flanked by Amy on his left and Marty to his right and held Amy's hand and pet Marty, who was sleeping.

Amy took a sideways glance and annoyingly blurted out, "What are you doing?"

Tom looked over at Amy. "What are you talking about?"

"Why are you petting Marty?"

"Are you serious?"

"Yes. You know I don't like it when you pet him. Your attention is split between me and him, and then your hands get dirty."

"Amy, you seriously have to chill. I think I'm capable of giving you attention and petting my dog at the same time."

"Actually, you're not. My therapist says you are using Marty as a shield between us and it's why you can't be in a committed relationship."

"Yeah, well I've met your therapist and he's a quackhole. He just wants to get into your pants."

"Don't talk like that! He's a good therapist and my advocate. He doesn't think you're ever going to be able to have a committed relationship because….

It was times like these that Tom wished he had severe tinnitus so that he wouldn't have to listen to her blabber on and on. Anything to drown her out. However, he didn't dare turn up the volume on the TV because he knew that would only escalate the situation.

Amy was thirteen years younger than Tom. She was a sexy blue-eyed blond with a Marilyn Monroe figure. Originally from Australia, she had come to America with a hunger for recognition, fortune, and fame. If Naomi Watts and Nicole Kidman could do it, so could she. She wanted to be an actress but had spent the last fifteen years fending for herself in full survival mode and not getting a chance to act or even refine her craft. Aside from appearing in a few short-lived reality shows and a straight to DVD horror movie, her resume was pretty light.

As with many struggling wannabe starlets in Hollywood, she had learned to use her charms and looks to finance her survival with guys willing to pay for arm candy. Tom had met her at the pool and took an instant liking to her and her Australian accent. It reminded him of Olivia Newton-John, whom he had a crush on in his formative adolescent years. He also deduced from conversations that she could only afford to be there because some Hollywood douchebag was picking up the tab and using it as his snack pad, and Amy was the snack.

Amy knew the rules and she played them well, but when the Hollywood douchebag wasn't around, Amy was hanging with Tom. She had an illusion that they might have a future together. Although he thought of himself as average looking, Amy kept insisting he was handsome and had natural sex appeal. She said she knew these things because she was an actress, so he didn't argue with her when it came to judging looks. The truth was he was also smitten with her even though she could drive him crazy at times. But she could also be a lot of fun in that she had a very imaginative sex life and Tom was always willing to play along. She never wanted to be herself in times of intimacy, which in itself was a blatant cry for intense therapy, but Tom wasn't a head shrinker and it wasn't his problem. It was her idiot therapist's problem.

Albeit a problem that would never get attention because Amy had never brought it up in the sessions from what she told him. Besides, he rather enjoyed the role play.

Amy finished her diatribe with "so please wash your hands."

Tom turned up the volume on a television news brief that caught his attention. A news anchor was covering a story about a Vietnamese couple that was fearful their daughter may have been kidnapped. The sixteen-year-old had gone missing in Simi Valley after she had left the local animal shelter where she volunteered on the weekends. A picture of a pretty young Vietnamese girl was displayed on the screen. The news anchor went on to say that police were investigating and asking for the public to contact them with any information. They had not ruled out foul play, including a possibility that she may have been abducted as part of the ever-growing sex trafficking industry. The news anchor went on to say that it was estimated that there were more than 4.8 million people in forced sexual exploitation working globally, and it was becoming more and more prevalent in the Southland.

"And in other news, another man died from apparent poisoning after taking a pill for erectile dysfunction that he bought at a local gas station. Authorities say that—"

Amy shut the TV off. "God, that is so horrible."

"No kidding. Imagine buying a pill so you can have some fun and then dying from it. Whoever did that is a sick fuck," countered Tom.

"No, not that. I mean the kidnapping. Makes me not even want to have kids." Tom sensed that Amy was truly upset and not just practicing her acting skills. She continued, "If I had a daughter who was kidnapped and I caught the guy, I would rip his nuts off and feed them to his dog." Tom raised an eyebrow. She then leaned over Tom, and to the dog said, "Sorry, Marty, no offense!" Amy looked at Tom, coyly smiled, then nuzzled closer to him. "So, Captain, how long is the flight going to be?" Tom grinned and reached with his hands to cup Amy's face and kiss her when she suddenly grabbed his wrists. "Wait. Go wash your hands." She bent toward the dog again. "Sorry, Marty, but I don't know where that tongue has been." She then turned to Tom. "But I do know where your tongue is not going to be if you don't get up and wash your hands."

Tom sighed as he got up from the couch and lumbered to the bathroom.

The Drop

Binh Nguyen pulled the van up to the back entrance of Hannah's Nail Spa in a back alley of a small strip mall in Simi Valley. It was 11 pm, but a full moon was casting a soft light in the alley which otherwise would have been completely dark. He hopped out of the van and limped to the back and waited. Binh was in his twenties, but the limp added a few years to him. He adjusted his shirt over his beltline, concealing a Glock-19 pistol snug in his pants. After a minute, the back door to the salon opened and an older, middle-aged man with white hair and a potbelly walked out and met Binh. He scanned the alley then nodded at Binh, who opened the back of the van, and the older man leaned in and looked inside.

Three young Vietnamese girls were ranging in ages from fifteen to seventeen sitting on the carpeted floor of the van, their clothes tattered and dirty. One of the girls was tied up, incoherent from being drugged. Binh shouted something to them in Vietnamese and two of the girls slowly got up and began to exit the van. The third girl remained, lying prone with her hands tied.

The older man smiled at them and helped them out. "Welcome to my world, my sweets." He stared at the third girl. She wasn't going anywhere in her condition, so he shut the van door.

After securing the van, Binh led them through the back door and into the nail salon. Inside, two elderly Vietnamese women began to clean the two girls with buckets of warm water and sponges and then gave them a new set of clothes and brushed their hair, all the while the older white-haired man watched. The young girls didn't resist.

When the older man was satisfied, he turned to Binh and gave him a small manila envelope. "Get the other one to the main house. She's going to be for the VIPs."

Binh nodded and spoke to the girls, who followed him out of the salon and back into the van.

The older man walked back in and nodded to the older ladies, who gathered their things and walked out the front door with him and locked up. The women went their separate ways and the older man got into a black Cadillac Escalade and drove out of the strip mall.

It's Vinyl, Man

Tom walked down the hallway to the garage door exit. He lived in a complex where each door was in a long hallway like a hotel. As he neared the end of his hallway, the door on the left, 414, opened and loud music echoed out into the hallway. Tom grimaced. He slowed to see if he could reverse direction, but it was too late. Randy Montrose was coming out of his doorway with a bag full of trash. Upon seeing him, Randy grinned and headed right for Tom.

"Hey, Tom. You gotta check this out."

"Hey, Randy, I'm running a bit late."

"This will only take a minute. You're going to love it."

Tom relented and followed Randy back into his unit. Randy put aside the garbage bags and went over to a vintage record player in the middle of the living room.

"Check this out!" he shouted above the loud music." "Black Dog" by Led Zeppelin was blaring out from the record player.

"Hey, you mind turning it down. We're gonna go deaf," Tom shouted.

"Oh, no no no. You need at least 150 decibels to blow someone's ears off." Randy picked up an old iPod which had a cord running to the record player. He swiped the dial and the volume decreased. "Isn't that sweet? I picked it up at an estate sale. It's an actual jukebox player from 1956 that you might find at a sock-hop juice joint or whatever those places were called. And check this out. I modified it so that I can control the volume from this old iPod." He held up the iPod and spun the dial on it, increasing the volume.

Tom grimaced as the music got louder. Suddenly, there was a loud pop from the jukebox and the music stopped. All you could hear was the faint sound of the needle riding on the grooves of the vinyl record.

"Ah, hell. I think I blew the speaker. Not perfect yet."

"Why would you want to jerry-rig an iPod to a record player?"

"I like melding the new with the old. Plus, I like vinyl."

"Vinyl sucks. I can't believe they've sold you millennials on it again."

"No way. Vinyl is it. I wish those Tower Record stores were still around. I would have loved to rummage through them. The cover art on the albums was incredible. Look at this." Randy reached down into a wicker bin and pulled up an album.

It was Boston's first album with the cover art depicting a guitar spaceship that encased a city in glass on the top and the blue flames shooting out from the soundhole of the guitar. The album did bring back some memories for Tom of doing just that—rummaging through a Tower Record store looking for cool album covers and sometimes buying a record solely based on the cover artwork. Boston was one of those albums.

Tom took the album from Randy and looked at it admiringly. "I gotta admit, that was the most fantastic cover. And it was a great album. You have good taste there, Randy."

Randy's face beamed at the compliment.

Hitting Hitsman

Born Thomas David Hitsman to a middle-class family in San Francisco, Tom was an only child who had gone to parochial schools growing up. His dad had been a sales rep for the airlines and his mom worked part-time at the local library. Although a bit of an introvert who liked paint-by-number artworks and model airplanes, he had a couple of close friends who lived on the same block as himself and they would do the usual kid stuff like riding bikes, playing catch, stealing hubcaps from the neighborhood cars and getting caught and grounded. An unremarkable childhood with no real hardships other than the typical bully bullshit that went on at school.

For some reason, two bullies at school, Gary Wargun and Danny Loftus, had zeroed in on Tom and would take turns sneaking up behind him and kidney punching him and then yelling victoriously, "Hitting Hitsman!" This led to a few scuffles, but mostly it got Tom thinking in a more devious manner on how to deal with these two assholes.

One day in the fourth grade, Tom went to the back of the classroom where the kids would put their coats on hooks and their lunches on the shelf above their coats. While the teacher was preoccupied with one of the other students, Tom found Wargun's coat and then reached above and grabbed his brown bag lunch. He checked the name on it first, confirmed it was his, and then threw it to the ground and stomped the shit out of it. As he swiveled his head to check on the teacher, he suddenly was face-to-face with Gary Wargun, who had probably snuck up to punch him.

Rather than panicking, Tom remained cool-headed and said, "Look at this!" He grabbed another lunch bag, threw it to the floor, and stomped on it, then another one and stomped on that one too. At this point mob mentality set in, and like dominoes bags of lunches hit the floor as Wargun swiped them off the shelf and exuberantly stomped on them. Meanwhile, Tom slipped away and hurried back up to the teacher and tugged on her sleeve. He pointed to the back of the classroom where Wargun was going ape-shit destroying his classmates' lunches.

The teacher's eyes narrowed, and she quickly strutted to the back and yanked him out of the closet by his ear and furiously dragged him down to the principal's office. It was a great win for Tom. He wasn't afraid of physically defending himself, but he learned if he was calm and cool he could find other ways to discreetly get even with these idiots. Eventually, the novelty of "Hitting Hitsman" wore off as bad shit seemed to be happening to them. They had a suspicion Tom might be behind it, but they couldn't prove it.

In high school, Tom discovered his first computer and he was hooked. He wasn't a partier or drinker, and he took some heat for it and eventually became a bit of a loner when his friends took to partying. Two of those friends became his nemesis when they joined forces with a rich kid because it gave them access to booze, pot, and other benefits that his money could garner. Tom's last two years in high school had been pretty miserable because of this unfortunate development.

In college, Tom chose computer science, studied hard, and made new acquaintances. Acquaintances were a better term than friends as he never really got too close to anyone. There were a few girls here and there as he never had to work too hard or go after them. They seemed to gravitate toward him of their own accord, but after finding out he wasn't the typical "fun" college guy they lost interest and moved on. By all accounts, Tom had matured into his tall lanky body and had filled out, and despite his pasty skin from being in front of a computer terminal 24/7, he looked like a young Pierce Brosnan. A distinction he was oblivious to but that was not lost on the young college girls in his classes. His parents attended his graduation, and he had a small celebratory get-together afterward with some of his acquaintances and the girl he was dating at the time.

After graduation, Tom worked at IBM where he designed code and eventually landed at a start-up in the late nineties called DoGondle, which he thought at the time was the most ridiculous name for a company. That ridiculous name ended up making him a wealthy man with his stock options and he decided to retire early and open his consulting firm. He didn't need the money, so he only worked by word of mouth and really to keep himself from going stir crazy.

Tom dabbled in Hollywood but lost a big chunk of money on a bogus film investment. Two brothers had started a production company and were using the Mel Brooks movie *The Producers* as their business model. The basic premise of the Mel Brooks comedy is that a producer could make a lot more money with a flop than a hit by overselling shares in the production because no one will audit the books of a play presumed to have lost money.

So, these two brothers applied this model to filmmaking. They would raise three million dollars for a movie and then produce it for six hundred thousand and pocket the rest of the money. The movie would be of such poor quality that it would never find a distributor and therefore never generate any funds let alone a profit margin, leaving the investors out of luck with no return on their investment. Tom was particularly bothered by this because he could afford to take a hit, but some of these people were average folk who had invested their entire retirement funds and all they received for their troubles was a t-shirt with the movie's title emblazoned on the front. It was a well-run scam, but unfortunately, the authorities wouldn't file charges because movie making was a speculative business so the scam ran on and on.

Tom had been excited about the prospect of being part of a movie because he enjoyed movies, but after that experience, he was soured on the entertainment business and decided Hollywood was full of self-deluded douchebags, sycophants, and crooks. He wasn't a vengeful person by nature, but he could justify a little payback on these two bozos, so he hacked their server and dropped a virus into it which essentially took them offline for a month and brought their call center to a grinding halt. It cost them quite a bit of money to repair. It was the least he could do.

Poolside

Amy and Tom were lounging by the pool enjoying the spring weather when she put down the book she was reading and turned toward him.

"Hey, I saw your invitation to your high school reunion. Are you planning on going?"

"No. I've never gone to one."

"Why not?" queried Amy.

"It was a mean-spirited class, and no one would remember me anyway."

"They would remember you if I was by your side. A hot Hollywood actress with a sexy accent. You'd be the envy of all the married guys."

Tom snickered. "That's probably true."

Amy turned toward him. "Ah c'mon, baby. It will be fun. I've never been to San Francisco. We could make it a romantic getaway weekend."

Tom frowned. "There isn't anyone I would want to see."

"The reunion will just be a stop along our romantic weekend. Besides, you should go back and flaunt your success in their faces." Amy leaned over and gave him a peck on the cheek. "And… there's something else."

"Oh? What's that?"

"That's the same weekend Larry wants me to go to Vegas with him to help him close some investors for his new project."

Tom lowered his sunglasses and looked into her spellbinding blue eyes. "What do you mean he wants you to help him close the investors?"

"You know, be his charming hot girlfriend who can flirt with them and sell them on the Hollywood dream. The underlying subliminal message is if you invest with Larry, you too can have hot Hollywood girls like this one." Amy waved her hand like Vanna White across her body.

"You know that guy is a real douchebag. I hope he doesn't make you do things you don't want to do."

"Hey, I never do anything I don't want to do." Amy leaned back into her chair and crossed her arms over her chest.

Tom realized he had hit a nerve. "I wasn't implying that you would do something like that, but I wouldn't put it past a guy like that to try and pimp you out. Look at that piece of shit Jeffrey Epstein. He got away with it for a long time right up until Hillary Clinton had him killed."

"What! Hillary Clinton had someone killed?"

Tom chuckled. "Well, if you believe all the conspiracy theories."

"Nice try on changing the subject. I can't believe you think I would allow someone to pimp me out."

They both sat in silence for a bit before Tom leaned over toward her. "I'm sorry. That came out wrong. I know you would never do anything against your will. You know what, fuck the douchebag. Let's go to San Francisco and have a fun weekend."

Amy looked at him with a big, bright smile. "Really?"

"Yeah, why not. And we can swing by the reunion and flip them all off," Tom said, smiling back at her.

"Ohhh, that's great, baby! That's going to be so much fun!"

Amy crawled onto his lounge chair and pressed her body on top of his and playfully kissed him all over his face. He winced as he felt a sharp stabbing pain in his stomach again. What the hell was that? Whatever that was, he didn't like it. No, he didn't like it at all.

Ventura Highway

The sun glistened off a dark satin grey Jaguar R coupe roaring up the Santa Barbara coastline on the 101 heading north toward San Francisco. The top was down, and Amy was sporting a big smile as the wind whipped through her golden hair. The Pacific Ocean was on their left, the mountains to their right. They came up behind two slower-moving vehicles, so as soon as they hit a straightaway section Tom looked over at Amy and grinned before shooting out into the oncoming traffic lane and sinking the accelerator.

"Zero to sixty in three-point-five seconds, baby!"

Amy felt herself sink into the leather seat as the Jaguar smoothly rocketed past the two slow-moving cars. "Wow that was hectic!" shouted Amy with a smile brighter than the sun.

"Yes, it was...hectic. I like that!"

Tom was enjoying himself. He rarely took his Jag out for a spin on city streets, but this was the perfect opportunity to enjoy it. His F-Type R Jag was powered by a 550-horsepower supercharged 5.0-liter V8. It was like being in a land rocket, and it came with a hefty price tag, but it wasn't the most expensive of high-end coupes.

Tom didn't flaunt his wealth, but this was the one luxury he had allowed himself to indulge in when he saw it in a showroom in Calabasas. He didn't even realize it was a Jaguar until he got up close. His everyday transportation was a BMW 4 series, and although it was a great car, it wasn't a Jag.

Tom put his cruise control on and set it to seventy-five miles per hour. He peered out at the ocean and watched the sun's rays hypnotically dance across its vastness. He felt a sense of peace and calmness. He remembered the song "Ventura Highway" by the 70's pop group America. "*Ventura Highway in the sunshine, where the days are longer, the nights are stronger than moonshine. You're gonna go I know. Cause the free wind is blowin' through your hair, and the days surround your daylight there, seasons crying no despair, alligators, lizards in the air…*" He had no idea what the lyrics meant, but accompanied by their acoustic guitars and tight harmonies they definitely captured the feeling of what he was feeling at that moment cruising up Ventura Highway. Until a twang of pain in his stomach snapped his attention back to the road.

He looked over at Amy. She had her eyes closed and was enjoying the warmth of the sun on her face. He admired her for a few moments then winced as another ripple of pain fluttered through his stomach. He opened up an Arnold Palmer and took a swig. Maybe he was hungrier than he thought and he just needed something in his stomach.

The Reunion

Amy and Tom checked into the Fairmont Hotel on Nob Hill, a world-renowned upscale hotel with glorious views of the beautiful San Francisco Bay and the majestic city skyline. After breaking in the bed with a round of bellboy and the soap star, they took showers, got dressed, and went to the Tonga Room for dinner. Amy loved the tiki-themed setting complete with a lagoon where a thatch-covered barge served as the floating stage for the Island Groove Band which performed Top-40 hits. The Polynesian-fusion cuisine was delicious, and the mai-tai's were among the best Amy had ever experienced—and she experienced quite a few of them.

After dinner, Tom and Amy walked through the hotel and up to the rooftop garden where they saw a bride and groom taking pictures with the San Francisco skyline as the backdrop. She leaned against Tom and put her head on his shoulder.

"Isn't that beautiful?" she said wearily as the mai-tai's seeped into her veins.

"Yeah...that's nice," replied Tom, feeling the effects of the long seven-hour drive up the coast. "Why don't we call it a night. We have some sightseeing to do tomorrow and the reunion tomorrow night."

Amy looked up at him with sleepy blue eyes, smiled, pulled him close, and gave him a kiss. They interlocked their arms and staggered back to their room.

After a day of sightseeing which had included Fisherman's Wharf, Coit Tower, Twin Peaks, and cable car rides, Tom and Amy arrived at Cabrillo High School in San Mateo. The guests were shuffled into the newly refurbished auditorium that had been recently paid for by Kent Lim.

Kent Lim still looked like the same little arrogant shit he had been in high school, just pudgier and greyer. As he walked to the podium, he grinned that cheese-rat grin of his and looked out into the bleachers, taking in the applause. He was wearing a dark blazer, royal blue shirt, grey slacks, and an ill-fitting short haircut. After a rehearsed sanctimonious speech about giving back to the school that had prepared him for the business world, he gave the peace sign and slinked off the podium. *Same old Kent,* Tom thought to himself. He was probably still living off his dad's money. *Once a lazy fucktard, always a lazy fucktard.*

The lady who introduced him came back on and reminded everyone that tickets would soon be on sale for the school's production of *Pirates of the Caribbean.* Kent cringed. He hated anything to do with pirates.

Gilman nudged Kent. “Hey, we should come back to town and see the play.”

“Fuck that shit. I hate pirates and I hate plays.” Kent continued strolling toward the bar.

“I like the ships, " Gilman said to himself. “Always thought I would have been a damn good pirate.” Moro, Kent’s huge Samoan bodyguard, grinned and shook his head at Gilman. “What? I would have been a great pirate! And I would have run you through with my trusty sword.”

Moro raised his eyebrow. “In your dreams.”

They both laughed as they trailed Kent to the bar.

The festivities began and the crowd splintered off into smaller groups catching up and chatting and ogling each other. As Tom made his way from one group to another, he felt as if all eyes were on him. He had not made much of an impression in high school, but now with his still youthful good looks and the stunning Amy by his side, he certainly stood out. He was catching up with Doug Petrie, whom he remembered as being a pretty cool guy, while his wife made small talk with Amy. Amy had chosen a gown she would have worn to the Academy Awards if she ever had the pleasure of attending. A beautiful blue sequined low-cut dress that amplified her feminine attributes and drew in male eyeballs like moths to a flame. She was sure she was causing a few retina burns and was devilishly happy about it. As Doug resisted asking Tom how in the world he landed Amy, Tom noticed Kent Lim and Darren Gilman hunkered together and looking over in his direction. Darren peeled away from Kent and started toward him.

Tom clenched his jaw and fists thinking this would be a good time to get even with Gilman for all the pain he had caused him in high school. Gilman was sporting thinning white hair and a beer belly, and although he still posed a formidable appearance, his face looked like that of a middle-aged man. Gilman cut a path through the crowd like he was still a linebacker and Tom was the quarterback.

Gilman pushed his way in front of Petrie and reached out and grabbed Tom's hand with a vice-like grip. He pumped his hand like a long-lost brother. "Tommy Hitsman! Look at you!" Gilman feigned a kidney punch, causing Tom to instinctively drop his elbow to block it. Gilman stopped short of making contact then grinned and pulled him into a bear hug. "Hitting Hitsman!" he shouted. He looked at Tom like it was a great memory they both shared.

Tom wanted to punch him in the face but he remained level-headed. "Darren. Long time. You still have the moves."

Gilman quickly shifted his gaze over to Amy and drank her in like a giant chocolate protein shake. "And who might this delicious beauty be? Tommy, is this your wife?" Gilman winked at Amy and reached in to grab her hand so as to kiss it, but Amy was quick to evade.

"Easy there, big guy. I don't want to chip a nail on those bruiser lips of yours."

Tom looked at Amy and smirked.

"What a sweet accent. British?"

"Australian. Much sexier than the Brits," retorted Amy.

"Darren, this is Amy. Darren was our star linebacker in high school. There are quarterbacks to this day still mending from his freight-train tackles, right, Darren?"

Darren ignored Tom and kept his eyes and grin on Amy. He looked her up and down like a lion about to take down a gazelle. "I don't see a ring on her finger, Tommy. You better put a ring on her or she might slip away."

"Tommy...has nothing to worry about." Amy leaned up and kissed Tom and winked at him.

Doug Petrie and his wife quietly slipped away while Gilman made a dog and pony show of himself. Then from across the room, Kent yelled out, "Darren! Let's go!" Kent either didn't recognize Tom or didn't give two shits, because he didn't acknowledge him and turned away.

Gilman nodded in compliance and then turned back to Tom. "Hey, Tommy, we are having a little private get-together tonight after the reunion. You and Amy should join us." Gilman slipped him a business card. "Text me at that number and I'll send you the address. It'll be great to catch up." Before Tom could answer, Kent yelled at Gilman again. Gilman's face turned bright red and his jaw clenched. "I'll see you two later tonight." He slapped Tom on the shoulder, pointed his finger at Amy, and swiftly spun and hurried back to Kent.

"What a tool," said Amy.

Tom nodded in agreement. "For all his bravado, he's still Kent's lapdog."

"What's the story with those two?" she asked.

"I'll tell you on our way to the party."

"Seriously? You want to go to that party and deal with that neanderthal?"

"Let's just say it piqued my interest."

What's Your Flavor?

Tom and Amy arrived at the Pullman Hotel in Redwood Shores, a newly developed area off the San Francisco Bay that had come into prominence because of Larry Ellison, who founded Oracle out on the shores some thirty years earlier.

They took the elevator to the penthouse, and upon entering were immediately hit with the wafting plume of marijuana and cigarettes. The lights were turned low and there were several men in casual business attire with drinks in hand comingling with several pretty women. As Tom took in the scene, he noticed the majority of the women were young and of Asian descent.

As they entered deeper into the room, Amy turned to Tom and said, "I feel like we just walked into a mail-order party for Asian brides."

"Yeah, no kidding."

A few eyes stared at the couple as they walked through the room. In particular, eyes focused on Amy. Suddenly, Darren shot through the crowd with a big grin on his face.

"Hey, you made it. C'mon, Kent is over in the back room." Darren gave Amy the once over and then turned and headed through the crowd ogling the women.

Tom and Amy followed. They entered the adjoining room and found Kent sitting on a long black leather couch with two women flanking him. On the table in front of him was a mountain of cocaine. Kent was smoking a joint when he looked up at Darren.

"Look who I ran into, boss. Tommy Hitsman!"

Kent looked at Darren and a slight smirk played on his chubby face. "Tommy. Long time." Kent leaned back into the sofa and motioned toward the cocaine. "Enjoy the party." He then essentially dismissed Tom as he turned his attention to the girls sitting with him.

Tom looked at Kent and at the rest of his entourage and then nodded, turned, and led Amy back to the main suite. Darren walked by his side and leaned in close to him and in a low voice said, "Don't mind Kent, he's stoned. Otherwise, he'd be excited to see you. Hey, I know Amy is quite the dish, but if you are interested in any other flavors let me know. There's plenty to go around." He flashed a big grin then peeled away from Tom into the crowd.

As Amy and Tom observed the interactions of the well-dressed men and the pretty young women, some of which looked underaged, they sensed that all was not right. The women had dead eyes and were not conversing with the men. It was very cordial in the main suite, but then you had Kent in a backroom doing blow and acting like a pimp daddy. He was also very indifferent in seeing Tom after all these years.

Amy turned to Tom and said, "I'm going to find the ladies' room, but then let's get out of here."

"Yeah, I've seen all I need to see."

Amy walked down a hallway in search of the bathroom while Tom stood by the front door waiting when Darren came up to him again.

"So, what do you think?"

"Think about what, Darren?"

"See anything you like?" Darren motioned toward a couple of girls huddled together.

"These girls are here for entertainment?" asked Tom, seeking confirmation for his suspicion.

"Yeah, Tommy. See all these dudes here? They've all paid a shitload of coin to be here. Some of these assholes are prominent members of society, yet here they are. But you're my guest so it's on me. But don't tell Kent. He can be a pain sometimes. You see that fish tank?"

Tom looked over at a large 100-gallon tank with colorful fish and decorative stones tucked in the corner.

"He's obsessed with his fish and travels with them everywhere he goes. Let me tell you, it's a pain transporting that goddamn fish tank everywhere."

"So, you work for Kent?"

"More like partners. But I make sure everything gets done. Like the head of operations."

Tom nodded. "Right."

"What exactly is your business?"

"You know…this and that. A little import-export and some small business holdings. So, what do you think? You want to try a different flavor, let me know. I can entertain Amy for you." Darren flashed Tom his toothy grin.

"Thanks. I'm good."

Darren looked him up and down, disappointment registering on his face. "Suit yourself. But this is a private party and we'd like to keep it that way. You know what I mean?" Darren looked Tom in the eye and smiled, but his eyes glared back a different meaning. One that Tom remembered from high school.

"Yeah. No worries, Darren. Your little secret is safe with me."

Darren stepped closer into Tom's private space. Tom could smell the alcohol emanating from his pores and breath. "Since you won't be partaking in tonight's festivities, I think it might be a good idea if you leave now."

Tom locked eyes with Darren and gave him his best Clint Eastwood glare. "Yeah, I think that sounds like a good idea." It wasn't exactly a Clint Eastwood line, but it was the first thing that came to mind.

"Can we please go now?" Amy reappeared next to Tom.

Tom and Darren glared at each other for a few moments before Tom broke off and grasped Amy's arm and spun and headed for the door. Amy looked back at Darren, who winked at her and said, "See ya, doll."

Once in the elevator, Amy exploded. "You were friends with these assholes in high school? You know they are up to no good, right?"

"First, no, I was not friends with them in high school—at least not these two idiots. Second, yes, I know they are up to no good. But it's none of our business."

"What!? You're not going to call the police? When I went to find the bathroom, one of those businessmen came out of one of the backrooms and I caught a glimpse of a girl inside. She looked just like the missing girl who was in the news the other night, and she looked scared. I tried to go into the room but some fucking big gorilla bodyguard wouldn't let me in. We have to call the police!"

"And the minute we do that, who do you think they are going to suspect called the cops?"

"I don't care. The minute we get back to the hotel I'm calling the cops on these criminals."

"Look, Amy, there were some prominent men in there and I have a feeling that calling the cops isn't going to do much other than stir up a beehive, and we are the ones that are going to get stung. Let's just drop…"

Tom clutched his stomach and hunched over in extreme pain before falling to his knees as a blanket of blackness covered him.

Gilman's Game

Darren Gilman shut the engine off on his black Cadillac SUV and speed-dialed Kent on his cell phone. It went straight to voicemail again. It wasn't unusual for Kent to be unreachable from time to time as he was usually stoned or getting laid by a tranny, but it had been a few days since he had returned from the San Francisco trip. Usually, Kent would want to know that the transfer of new girls went on without a hitch. Gilman was the operations manager for KNLM, which meant he was the hands-on guy for the sex trade portion of the nail salon business.

What had started as a semi-legitimate nail salon business for Kent Lim's father had turned into a very lucrative sex trafficking operation once Kent had taken it over. It didn't happen overnight, but within ten years it had become much more lucrative than the nail salon that was now just a front for sex trafficking. Now after fifteen years it was a multi-million-dollar operation ranging from San Francisco to Southern California. Darren had always admired Kent, mostly for his money, and had always been like a pilot fish around a shark, eating the scraps. But he was loyal and a trusted confidant since high school, so Kent had kept him employed.

Through the years Darren had worked in various positions for Kent and was responsible for starting the sex trafficking part of the business on his initiative when one of the nail salon girls had propositioned him because she needed more money. She took a big chance propositioning the boss, but she sensed it was his weakness, and when Gilman took the bait the following week she offered up her younger co-worker. That got Gilman's wheels turning, and he did his research. Once he explained to Kent how it could work and how much money could be made, Kent gave Gilman his blessing and let him loose so long as he was hands-on and took care of any problems. Gilman was more than happy to take on the responsibility, and he took himself off the books and the radar.

Aside from being a sex and pornography addict, Gilman knew that using the nail salons as a cover was brilliant. Normally massage parlors were the source of sex trafficking, and when Kent had suggested opening up a Jack Shack, Gilman had talked him out of it and pointed out the obvious. That was just asking for trouble. The nail salons were a legit business and less suspect to cops as far any illegal sex activities. Hygiene—well, that was another problem, but that was a health code violation and not a "you're going to prison violation" for being a sex trafficker. So, the business plan had worked and Gilman had become a wealthy man.

The girls would work in the salons during the day and then be sent out to clients at night. If the girls were young, pretty, and special, they would be kept in safe houses and forgo the nail salon work. These girls were for special upscale clients, and there were several safe houses logistically located throughout Southern California with a couple in Northern California in the San Francisco Bay Area. Southern California was privy to the depraved entertainment industry and corrupt politicians more so than Northern California, so he had set up the majority of houses throughout the Southland. Gilman had a small crew that helped him run the business, but he also often traveled to inspect the houses himself and to sample some of the goods. He had always had a thing for Asian girls, so you could say he loved his job more than a fat diabetic kid in a candy shop.

Gilman got out of his SUV and walked up the drive to his front door. He lived in a quiet neighborhood in Thousand Oaks, California, where everyone including the cops drove SUVs. He unlocked the door and walked into his craftsman-style house. The decor of the house was a pawn shop specialty—mostly because he loved pawn shops and had bought many of his furnishings from them. He wasn't about to go buy furnishings from IKEA and then spend eight hours trying to figure out how to put some flimsy wooden piece of furniture together. Who had time for that nonsense?

He went to his wet bar and poured himself a Glenfiddich which he downed in one swallow. "Ahhh. Smoother than butter on a baby's butt," he said out loud and chuckled.

Gilman then sauntered into the kitchen and opened the fridge looking for a snack. He grabbed a couple of slices of salami and pepper jack cheese and rolled them up together and stuffed them into his large mouth. Upon reaching his office, he plopped down in his chair and turned on the computer. First, he checked his email for any pertinent messages and to see if Kent had contacted him, and after going through all of them he decided to check the dark web. A majority of his regular sex business clients reached him through the various bulletin boards and forums. Most of his clients were upscale gentlemen that by most standards were considered stalwart pillars of society. But he had learned everyone has secrets and desires. Even the rich and influential one-percenters of the country were not immune from occasionally dipping their peckers into the backstreets of society.

Then he Googled the news article on the latest man who had died after ingesting a poison-laced male enhancement pill. He liked to find out who it was and if he had a family and other personal details. He would look them up on social media and go through the victim's photos and read their last posts. He sipped his scotch and fervently consumed the details on the latest victim. He was married, had a wife and two kids, and was fifty-six years old. He was a plumber and had his own small business. Gilman smiled as he perused the photo albums and the tribute his family had posted and how sickened they were that some horrible monster in China had poisoned the pills. The pills were, after all, made in China.

Gilman had started the side business of distributing these sexual enhancement pills that could be found in gas stations and adult bookstores a few months back. Turns out it was easy to become a distributor. You could just buy the packaging from a factory in China and then fill the pill with whatever you wanted to. Baking soda, sugar—sometimes rat poison. Out of a batch of a hundred, he would gleefully put some rat poison mixed with baking soda in one of the pills. It was something he had recently started doing just for shits and giggles. He couldn't believe how easy it was to get the packaging and then distribute them to various outlets. He had been very careful to cover his tracks. So far, three men had died from his extracurricular activities. He figured after this final batch he would lay low for a while. No sense in getting caught. He knew that sales would probably drop as men would stop buying the pills, and he regaled in the thought that it would affect China more than anything. He wasn't a fan of China, the CCP, or their communist policies, but he liked the Chinese people—especially their delicious food at Panda Restaurant or the PickUp Sticks in Studio City. So, a little bad PR for the CCP was ok by him.

Gilman snickered knowing that the pills didn't work since he wasn't adding anything but sugar and baking soda to them. He wished he could see the faces on the men that had been duped by his placebo pills, holding their pathetic unresponsive puds in their fist. Oh well, you can't have everything. He continued scrolling through the photos and poured himself another scotch. So much to do.

Seriously, Doc?

Tom sat on the barely cushioned steel gurney. He looked out the window at the parking lot below then back at the wall in front of him. With the exception of the cool guitar paintings adorning the wall, it was a typical doctor's office. He pulled out his cell phone and dialed Amy again. After they returned home Amy insisted he go to a doctor. So, here he was, and there she was in Vegas with the douchebag producer at some film premiere. Tom had acted like it wasn't a big deal if she went away, but it did bother him. The phone rang a few times and went straight to voicemail. He listened to her sexy accent right up to the beep and then hung up. He knew she probably wouldn't answer, and he wasn't sure what he would say anyway. Maybe that he was at the doctor's office. He sighed and put his phone back in his pocket as the door opened and the doctor entered. They had done a colonoscopy a few days earlier and removed a blockage and done a biopsy. He was there for the follow-up.

The doctor sat down in front of him sporting a stone face. He looked down at the document he was holding in his hand. "There's no way to say this other than to say it. We got the biopsy results back from the mass that was in your colon.

It's positive for cancer. I'm going to refer you to an oncologist and he will do a more in-depth test and put together a course of treatment."

There was a long pause as Tom's brain tried to register what he had just heard. "So, it's curable?"

"It depends on the stage. If it's stage one we can work with it, and if it's stage four, well, there are meds to make you more comfortable."

"How long would I have if it was...stage four?"

"Six months. But it's hard to say for sure. Just go to the oncologist and he will take it from there." The doctor paused for a moment, then mustered a consoling face. "I'm sorry, Tom. If you have any questions you can call my office."

Tom nodded and then the doctor got up and exited hastily. Tom looked out the window at the parking lot below and could see the heat shimmer off the parked cars.

The Yearbook

Sunlight streamed through the swaying pine trees and dappled the wooden deck with a golden hue that Southern California was famous for in TV shows and commercials. Tom sat on a deck chair wearing sunglasses and a Dodgers baseball cap and navy-blue t-shirt and jeans. Marty was lying next to him basking in the afternoon sun as well. Despite the sunny day, Tom was in a dark mood. Why did he have to get sick? So many assholes, scumbags, and corrupt people in the world and they would continue enjoying their rancid lives while his life would soon be ending. The more he dwelled in the catacombs of despair the angrier he got.

He was angry for not having done a colonoscopy years earlier as had been recommended by his doctor but mostly angry that it happened to him instead of his neighbor. Or that piece of shit Bill Maher. Tom thought about his recent trip to San Francisco and the high school reunion. He had finally talked Amy out of calling the authorities by explaining to her that it could ruin her acting career if she got tangled up in a mess with those guys—especially if she ended up dead. That got her attention, and she didn't mention it again on the entire drive back down to Southern California.

On his lap, Tom had his old high school yearbook he had dug out from his storage unit after searching through countless cardboard boxes. He wasn't sure why he had held on to the yearbook since he had hated high school, but now he was glad he had saved it. He blew the dust off the cover and flipped it open and thumbed through the pages, some of which were yellowed and stuck together, looking at photos of football games, basketball games, dances, theatrical productions, and various high school clubs. He remembered some of the faces and some he had no idea who they were. He recognized a couple of the teachers and wondered if they were still alive. Most of the teachers he remembered as being cool and fair. No sadists like the nuns from his grammar school years.

Well, there was one sadistic coach who used to torture his charges by lining them up against the chain-link fence and throwing baseballs at them full force. But he was the exception. Sometimes he would chase them around the block in his car. Tom was pretty sure that the character Billy Bob Thornton played in the movie *Mr. Woodcock* was probably based on this guy. God willing that sadistic prick had wound up on the wrong end of a foul ball at a baseball game.

Tom continued flipping pages and finally got to the headshot section of the graduating class. First up was Paul

Clark. He studied the smug smile on his adolescent face. What a dick. He remembered back to a day when he had been talking to another student and Paul had come up behind him and without any warning viciously shoved him from the back, giving Tom whiplash. To this day his neck still creaked and hurt from time to time. Tom reached for a black magic marker. He drew a couple of horns on top of Paul's head and then drew a big black "X" across his face. Even though Paul had not been at the reunion, Tom was sure he was still somehow involved with Kent and Gilman. Next up was Kent Lim. He drew a small "X" across both eyes and mouth and then a giant "X" across his entire face. Kent was still a smug drug-addicted jerkoff, and now he was a kingpin of some sort. Although their meeting in San Francisco had been brief, Tom sensed evilness emanating from Lim. Plus, all the anguish he had suffered in high school was because of Lim.

The page flipping continued until he came to Darren Gilman. The final ratpack member of the Lim entourage. He took his magic marker and blackened the two front teeth on Darren's photo. Although Gilman had tried to win his favor at the reunion, he had failed.

Tom never liked these three idiots, but now that he knew they were most likely sex traffickers, he disliked them even more. He felt a deep fury rise within himself. Why should they get to live and he has to die? The world wasn't fair and he knew it, but maybe there was a way to even it out. With his new diagnosis, Tom now had nothing to lose, right? He thought about that for a moment.... *Nothing to lose.* The doctor said he would most likely be dead in six months.

Going to the cops was an option, but would be too easy and would put him on their radar. Hacking them would be easy as well and may slow them down, but most likely would not stop them. Plus, Tom wasn't sure how they were running the organization and if it was an online enterprise. Killing them? Well, that was an interesting thought that flickered through his brain. A very interesting thought. The more Tom lingered on this crazy idea, the less crazy it seemed. He was surprised that he wasn't tossing his lunch. Could he kill someone? No, not some random shmoe. But could he kill these three guys? He felt a faint surge of energy shoot through his body. Almost imperceptible, but it was there.

Shutting the yearbook, Tom took a sip of his Arnold Palmer. He really liked those. He looked down at Marty lying next to him and watched him peacefully sleeping. "You know I love you, right, buddy? I'm going to make sure you're taken care of when it's time for me to go. You won't have to worry about a thing. But I'm gonna miss you, buddy." Tom continued to watch his dog steadily breathing, his furry chest rising up and down. Tom closed his eyes, slowly swaying in his chair to the beat of the wind. "If I was the wind, life would be a breeze," he said softly to no one in particular.

Chatty Norman

Gilman boarded his flight from San Francisco to Burbank, California. He hated San Francisco with all the homeless feces decorating most of downtown and was glad to be out of that overcrowded cesspool of a city and on his way back home. He had flown back up to go see the *Pirates of the Caribbean* and had enjoyed it. He especially liked the giant pirate ship prop that the kids had made that would swing onto the stage as if riding the waves. He had not told Kent about his quick trip and decided to keep it that way.

His seat was 14F, next to the emergency exit, which gave him extra legroom. He always tried to get the seat next to the emergency exit because of the extra legroom. And because in the event of an emergency he would be more than happy to help open the hatch and be the first one out.

Now he only had to worry about who would be sitting next to him. Would it be some overweight frenzied mom with a little screaming crumb snatcher or a turban-wearing terrorist on his way to a clandestine meeting with a political operative working on the deconstruction of America from the inside out? Either way, he was sure it wouldn't be a hot

Catholic high school girl. The chances of this happening on a plane ride were slim to none. Then a nice surprise happened.

A very nice-looking woman sat next to him. She was a brunette with a Bettie Page-style haircut framing her face. He guessed she was in her mid-forties but in good shape. She was tanned and had deep brown chocolate-colored eyes, sharp cheekbones, and full lips. She was wearing a maroon tight-fitting shirt with a plunging neckline giving him a glimpse of what lingered beneath the soft cotton. She wore a blue jean skirt that showcased her tanned, muscular calves and perfect pedicured feet in white sandals. *Very nice for an older broad*, he thought to himself. He had been spoiled by the young merchandise he handled, but this…this was not bad. It had been a long time since he had bumped uglies with a woman closer to his age. Maybe she was into some rough play. Although he was determined to keep a low profile on the flight, he thought this might be worth the risk. He also didn't spy a wedding ring.

As the woman settled into her seat Gilman saw she had a book he had spotted at the entertainment stand in the terminal, so he used that as his opening. Or at least he tried to. Just as he was about to engage her in flirtatious banter an overweight bald guy in a Hawaiian shirt and vomit-colored cargo shorts sat next to her in the aisle seat. Right away this was an affront to Gilman because he detested the Hawaiian shirt and cargo pants look because it was the uniform du jour of IT specialists across corporate America. Wannabe hipsters intimating that they were on vacation at work because they were so special and brilliant it wasn't really work, it was a vacation. That and their stupid beards. *When did the whole beard thing become a thing?* he wondered. He had recently read a study that indicated men with beards had more germs than dogs. *I guess the bearded millennials had missed that memo*, he thought to himself.

As far as Gilman was concerned, there were only two circumstances when a man should sport a long scraggly beard. If you were a Jihad terrorist or in ZZ Top. At least this guy didn't have a beard, but he did have a mouth. He wasn't in his seat more than a millisecond when he turned to her and started a conversation.

The man launched into a story about how he had been monitoring his son's video game playing and he felt the gun-centric games were not suitable for him at his age, and then began to describe a variety of popular first-person shooter games along with the objective and strategy behind each one. Now at this point, he had not yet bothered to ask her any personal questions nor let her interject, and he was loud and obnoxious and unfazed that the flight attendants were trying to convey the safety measures on the Airbus.

Fifteen minutes into the flight, the guy was still chattering nonstop, and the woman who had the restraint of a statue was still attentively listening to him and occasionally getting one word in for clarification on one of his stories. This guy was the most self-absorbed asshole Gilman had ever had the displeasure of being in close proximity to, and it was all he could do to keep from reaching across the woman's ample breast and ripping out this guy's vocal cords.

This bald turd was supposedly a public speaking expert who was on his way to give a seminar in Burbank. He was also rich and had over 180 financial advisors but didn't want to spend the extra hundred bucks on first class. What the fuck!? Gilman had enough and tapped the lady on the arm, indicating he needed to exit.

The fat rat continued to talk as he stood up to make room for Gilman, who clenched his jaw as he squeezed past him and headed to the bathroom at the rear of the plane. He entered and sat on the toilet trying to control his now rising blood pressure. Sitting on the cramped toilet, he tried to take the edge off his rage over this retarded fat fuck with no sense of social graces that had ruined his flight and any chances of hooking up with the woman next to him.

Gilman had killed before. Although it had been an act that he justified as in the line of duty for Kent, he had enjoyed it. It had been one of his minions he used for transporting the girls who had tried to make some money running a few of the girls himself and keeping the profits. When Gilman got wise to him, he took a baseball bat to his head and spilled his brains. He also broke the kneecap of his accomplice but let him live. Binh was now a very devoted minion. The police had written it off as a gang-related death and closed the case much to Gilman's delight. Gilman was never even a suspect. Getting away with murder thrilled him. Ever since that first kill, he knew if the opportunity arose again he wouldn't hesitate. He had read a few books on the subject of serial killers, trying to understand the mindset.

He knew from research that most predatory subs that grew into full-on homicidal serial killers had usually started by torturing animals when they were kids and gradually gained experience as they went from animals to humans. He also knew that he was not a pathetic serial killer like that pussy Dahmer, who couldn't control his urges, as is usually the case with these nutjobs. Nope. He knew exactly what he was doing and was in complete control of his urges, instincts, and emotions. There were a couple of times when he wanted to kill Kent, but he knew that was just a fleeting thought usually following one of Kent's temper tantrums. The little prick had been good to him over the years, and they had been friends since high school so there was a sense of loyalty that comes from that high school bond.

Turbulence knocked Gilman out of his reverie. He got off the toilet, opened the lavatory door, and stepped out next to the small galley at the back of the plane. The flight attendants were going down the aisle passing out snacks, so he helped himself to a bag of peanuts and a can of Coke that was sitting on the rack behind him. He could see that the blowhard was still talking a mile a minute with the woman seated next to him. He felt bad for her. He started to wonder if this ass-bite suffered from some kind of brain malfunction like serial killers did, only in his case, instead of having the urge to kill, he was simply afflicted with the urge to be a social moron. It didn't matter because he wasn't going to go back to his seat. Instead, Gilman spotted an empty aisle seat two rows up and he sidled up to it and sat down. The passenger in the middle seat had his eyes closed and earphones on and didn't even notice.

From this vantage point, Gilman watched for the next fifteen minutes as the social moron kept his head tilted toward the woman and spat out some more mundane personal pontifications. The guy didn't stop talking. His bald head just kept bobbing up and down like a buoy in a harbor. How could she endure it without slicing his throat? How could the flight attendants not rally to her defense and eject him from the plane at thirty thousand feet or at least put him in the luggage hold? Gilman wasn't sure why this jerkoff was irritating him so much, but he knew that he couldn't let this go. Something had to be done. He pondered for a few minutes and decided. The bald-headed bobber had to die.

Making New Plans, Stan

It had been a few weeks since the diagnosis and the trip to San Francisco, and the days seemed to be running together for Tom. Upon his return, Tom had buried himself in research and was dissecting every aspect of his nemesis' lives. He was enjoying his newly made plans and was impressed with how many different ways one could think up in terms of killing another human being. Although to be fair, he didn't regard them as humans anymore. It was a conscious mind shift on his part to help him carry out his plan. He was managing the pain with hydrocodone, and luckily it had been working.

His relationship with Amy had cooled off since their return from San Francisco when he had refused to turn in his sicko pals, and she had also been spending more time with the douchebag producer who had come into some money. Most likely from ripping someone off. Tom had pondered telling Amy about his plans to kill the three amigos, but he feared her reaction would be one of sheer delight. He didn't want to end up getting caught because she might accidentally tell someone simply out of exuberance.

Closing his laptop, Tom sunk into his couch. He was as prepared as he could be. Another girl had disappeared in the time he had been back. Tom had also researched the billionaire Jeffrey Epstein, who was considered by some to be the world's most prolific pedophile. Jeffrey Epstein was a New York-based financier with high-profile ties to the world's ultra-wealthy and powerful. Accused of sexually abusing many underage girls, Epstein was finally caught and charged for soliciting a minor for prostitution in Florida in 2008 and became a registered sex offender. Of his eighteen-month prison sentence, he served thirteen months. In July 2019, Epstein was arrested again—this time on federal charges of sex-trafficking minors. While awaiting trial, he was found dead in his jail cell on August 10, 2019. He was pals with many celebrities, politicians, kings, you name it. Between his private jet, Lolita Express, and his Sex Island, there was no way he could be allowed to go to trial. Therefore, he was found dead in his cell while on suicide watch. Ironically, the cameras were not working the day he died. Tom figured, as did many others, that someone up high had taken him out.

He didn’t think Kent and his cronies were anywhere in the same league, but he wasn’t sure how extensive their sex trafficking network was or who the clients were at this point. Not yet. During his research, Tom found that Paul Clark was involved, but only as the financial man as far as he could tell. It didn't make a difference. He soon would be dead. And what a glorious death it would be.

Vocal Redaction

"Boy, can you talk. You ear-fucked that poor woman sitting next to you for over an hour and a half, and I bet you didn't even get her name because you never gave her a chance to say a word. You don't care about anything but hearing your loud, obnoxious voice spewing your boring opinions and personal crap that no one cares about." Gilman looked at the ID in his hand. "Norman. You're a fuckface idiot. The fact that you make a living giving seminars on public speaking is an insult to the universe." Gilman slipped the ID into his back pocket.

Norman Pittman's limbs were tied to a pallet that was secured to a wall. He had a gag around his mouth preventing him from speaking. Gilman walked up to Norman and ripped the tape off his mouth. Norman spit out a blood-soaked hanky, coughed, sputtered, and then hissed at Gilman. A spray of blood shot out. Norman's eyes grew wide, his face full of rage as he hissed like a wildcat at Gilman again. Gilman laughed and Norman hissed even louder than sputtered and coughed. A glob of blood shot out of his mouth and onto the floor in front of him. Norman winced in pain.

Gilman reached into his coat pocket and pulled out what looked like soggy, short noodles about an inch in length and held them gingerly. They were blood-soaked. He held them up in front of Norman's face. "These, Norman, are your vocal cords. It's the reason no sound is emanating from that obnoxious mouth of yours." Norman looked incredulous at Gilman. He hissed again and a light spray of blood shot out. "You can do that all you want now but you won't be annoying anyone else with your incessant chatter—ever. The world's ears are once again safe and sound." Gilman laughed out loud at his joke. "I had a good chance of hooking up with that MILF sitting next to me until you showed up. Normally I like 'em a little younger, but she was a sexy lady, right, Norman? I never thought I'd be cockblocked by another man's mouth, but there's a first time for everything. And a last time." Gilman walked up to Norman and dropped the stringy vocal cords into the front pocket of his Hawaiian shirt and then patted them, making sure he smooshed them up nicely.

"Consider yourself lucky. I was going to kill you, but this actually turned out to be a lot more fun for me. Oh, and remember, I know where you live, so if you talk, oops, if you write down any information about me to the pigs, I'll come and find you, and next time it won't be your vocal cords I cut off. You got that, fuck face?"

Norman wearily looked at him and nodded yes. Gilman looked him up and down. He liked what he saw. He pulled out his cell phone and snapped a photo of pathetic Norman.

"Today is Saturday, so I imagine someone will find you on Monday morning. Try not to bleed out between now and then." Gilman spun and headed toward the other end of the warehouse and let himself out.

Darkness Revisited

Three Months Later

"Ok, let's rock and roll. Oh wait, I almost forgot." Tom aimed a little remote control off to the side, and suddenly the opening guitar riffs to AC/DC's "Highway to Hell" exploded from a boombox somewhere in the darkness. "Thought you'd enjoy this blast from the past since it was one of Lim's favorite tunes to crank up while cruising with that cheese-rat grin of his." Paul pissed himself. Tom got a breath away from Paul's sweaty face. "Goodbye, Paul. This has been by far the best high-school reunion ever."

Paul moaned at the top of his voice as Tom pulled the pin from the fire extinguisher and squeezed the handle.

Down in the Alley

Tom exited the warehouse and stepped into the dark alley. The night was cold and brittle, but there was an electrical charge running through his veins. Who knew that revenge decades later could be so…exhilarating?

Tom scanned the area and determined it was safe. He had on dark clothing and a black baseball cap tucked down low in case he had missed any nearby cameras that might catch him, even though he was pretty sure that was not the case. He had done his due diligence and picked a remote warehouse near the docks. Tom walked over behind a garbage container where he had parked his rented Ford Taurus. After getting in, he checked the rearview mirror and surrounding area to make sure there was no one around and opened the glove compartment and took out a prescription bottle of hydrocodone, twisted the top off, and popped one into his mouth. Just one to take the edge off the pain. He didn't like taking any kind of narcotics, but he required some kind of pain management, and these did the trick. He admittedly knew these little pills could make you a little spacey, so he had made sure he was off the painkillers for his reunion with Paul. He also knew they were addicting and supposedly half the country was addicted and overdosing if you believed the current administration.

The entire ordeal had taken a couple of hours from the time he had snuck up on Paul, injected him with ketamine, dumped him into the trunk of his car, transported him, and inflated him up like a piñata with the extinguisher. The pain was back now and ruining the high he was feeling, and he needed to dull it. Tom looked in the mirror, held his gaze for a moment, then looked away. He had pulled it off, and it had been easier than anticipated. Of course, this was the culmination of months of planning and recon, but it had gone about as smoothly as it could have gone when committing murder. Jacked up on adrenaline and pain, Tom put the car in gear and drove out of the alley and onto the city streets.

Tom's plan was to travel north on I-95 from Baltimore to Philadelphia and stay overnight at a motel and catch his flight the next morning back to California. He had meticulously planned this trip to elude any chance of detection and apprehension. That would not be good. He still had two more high school chums to catch up with, and he very well intended on completing those "reunions." Especially after this one had given him such a buzz. Tom had rented the car with a fake ID and bought the airline ticket with a second fake ID. All in all, Tom had spent a little over ten grand on three fake IDs, all with corresponding birth certificates, passports, and credit cards. It was the "Full Z" package available on the dark web.

As Tom drove up I-95 he thought about high school. What a messed-up place high school could be. You had your jocks, your brainiacs, your nerds, your stoners, your cheerleaders, your hot girls, your musicians, your prodigies, and your "invisibles"—basically, your normal kids who didn't fit into any of the groups. You were just there. Tom had been one of those "invisibles." *Not tonight*, he thought.

Tom took a deep breath and settled in and put the car on cruise control as traffic was moving swiftly at this time of night. He connected his blue tooth to the car stereo system and picked Elvis Presley for his travel music. First up on the playlist was a song called "We're Gonna Move." A simplistic yet catchy tune about moving out of a dilapidated house. It was from his first movie, *Love Me Tender*. What stood out about "We're Gonna Move" was that despite the lame lyrics, such as, "There's a crack across this ceiling," Elvis brought a playful, bouncy exuberant vocal to the song that got you singing along. You believed him when he sang in his baritone, "We're gonna move to a better home."

It wasn't as bad as some of the other shit songs he would end up singing during his movie years. With the exception of a few standouts such as "Return to Sender," "Viva Las Vegas," and "Can't Help Falling in Love," you could basically just discard all the movie soundtracks and not even blemish his outstanding career. By now it was pretty well known that his manager, Colonel Tom Parker, was key in Elvis's early career, but in the later years treated him like a freak in a carnival show and put his interests above his clients' interests. Tom thought to himself, *If I had a time machine I might consider going back and paying the ol' Colonel a visit and feeding him a fire extinguisher.* Maybe just half a tank. Enough to get him to give Elvis the creative freedom he needed to stay alive.

"You fuck with the King, I fuck with you, Colonel."

"Hound Dog" came on next, and Tom drove on through the dark night singing along with the King, feeling the effects of the pain pill kicking in, his euphoria as bright as the red taillights flickering on the highway.

A Little Help from Your Friends

Randy was fiddling with one of his gadgets when there was a knock on the door. Since he wasn't used to getting visitors, he was curious as to who it could be, so he looked through his peephole. He smiled and opened the door.

"Hey, Tom! I haven't seen you around too much lately. How's it going? Oh, and thank you for what you did with that crazy gal."

"Did that work out?"

"Sure did. I never heard from her again. Thanks again. So, what have you been up to? You want a beer?" They moved into the living room.

"No, I'm good. But I have a question for you. How difficult would it be for you to make another one of those contraptions that incorporates an iPod and a high-end tuner? Preferably one that can really crank out the volume through headphones."

"For you? No problem."

"How long will it take?"

"I have to find the components, assemble and test it out.... So, about a week or two."

"Can you make sure the components can't be traced back to you?"

Randy looked at him quizzically. "Yeah, I can do that."

"Is a thousand enough to get started?" Tom gave him a wad of cash.

Randy looked at Tom a little surprised but grabbed the cash and shoved it into the front pocket of his pants. "Yeah, that should be fine. Thanks. Who exactly is this for if you don't mind me asking?"

"Let's just say it's going to be a surprise for an old friend." Tom started for the door. "I'll check in with you next week. Thanks."

"Hey, you want to stick around and watch something on Netflix?" asked Randy.

"Thanks for the offer but I have a ton of work. Next time."

Randy nodded as Tom exited the apartment. Randy walked over to his kitchen table and then pulled the wad of cash out of his pocket and laid it on the table. He took a sip of a beer and started to count the bills.

Tom walked into his apartment and was greeted by Marty. He went into the kitchen and into the treat basket, which Marty instantly recognized and began turning in circles. Tom filled one of Marty's Kongs with various treats and placed it on the floor. Marty began to push it around with his nose trying to get the treats out.

Tom left him to have his fun and went over and turned on the TV. He settled on a news channel and sat back and watched with the sound off. On the screen were images of burning cities from riots carried out by what he thought of as professional protestors, called BLM and Antifa. He wasn't much into politics, so he wasn't even sure what they were protesting. They just seemed to be having a good old time looting and destroying at the expense of the citizens. He flipped to another news channel. He didn't expect he would see anything about Paul, but it didn't hurt to take a quick look. He wondered if the cops had found the body yet. He had been very careful to make sure nothing could be traced back to him, including the warehouse where he had his reunion with Paul. His knee bounced up and down nervously. He was anxious to get to Kent before word reached him of Paul's demise.

Hawthorne

Detective Dale Hawthorne rewound the tape once more. He was looking for any possible clues he could spot to help him get an idea of who had abducted Paul Clark. Paul had been missing more than a week now and no ransom had come in for his return. His car had been found in the parking lot of CVS pharmacy with the driver's-side door open.

The cops had worked the scene and reviewed video from the two cameras that were installed in and around the premises and parking lot. They had found one camera had just barely caught the incident, but the distance was about ten yards from the camera, the footage from the surveillance camera blurry and grainy. It showed Paul as he reached his car after leaving the pharmacy. As he opened the door, a subject in dark clothing came up behind him and grabbed him, wrapping one arm around his neck. It looked like he had placed his other hand over Paul's face, and after a brief struggle Paul had gone limp and the subject had dragged him out of frame.

Hawthorne guessed he had been drugged. He estimated the attacker was about six-foot given that Clark was about five feet nine inches tall. One of the other cameras had caught several vehicles leaving the area, but it was impossible to tell exactly what make and model, and the license plates weren't visible. And if the vehicle had exited through the back of the complex and not the main entrance, they wouldn't have any footage at all.

"You've been staring at that fuzzy video for hours now. You're gonna go blind." Natalie Martinez was standing behind Hawthorne. She was petite and looked a lot like Jennifer Lopez with her hair scooped back and her almond skin. She had been in the detective bureau for six months, and although she wasn't cocky, she was self-assured.

"You're probably right," Hawthorne said. "Did forensics find anything?"

"No, nothing," Martinez responded.

"Did they check the dumpsters?"

"Yes, for the fiftieth time. The scene was clean, Dale."

Dale Hawthorne had been a cop for over twenty years and was currently in his fourth year in the detective bureau. It was usually a rotating two-year assignment, but he was good at what he did and closed a lot of cases, so the two years had come and gone and the brass unofficially extended his assignment even if a few of the silver badges murmured from time to time. But he was well-liked and still went to the local cop bar to have drinks with the rank and file so there wasn't any real animosity.

He looked like your typical all-American cop, a-la Josh Brolin, and kept himself in decent shape by hitting the bag and daily runs. He had once gotten in a fight with a Hell's Angel drug dealer who had grabbed him by the ears and rammed his knee into his face repeatedly and nearly killed him. Dale swore he would never be at a physical disadvantage again and had hit the weights hard after that incident.

Dale pushed back from the desk and stretched his sore neck. "Let's take a drive back over to the wife and see if she's remembered anything that might help us."

"Are you going to show her the video?" asked Natalie.

"We probably shouldn't. But maybe she'll see something we haven't."

Natalie looked at him dubiously.

Dale sighed. "Yeah, probably not."

What Dale Hawthorne did know was that he was going to show Paul's wife the most horrific video she would ever have to watch.

Kent

Kent was sitting at his office desk shouting into the phone in his high-pitched shrill voice. "No! I didn't feed it anything else, just the food you sold me. No, no, no, you listen to me! The fish is defective and now it's floating around like a flaccid penis! I don't care about your store policy! If I don't get a new fish delivered to me free of charge today, I'm going to go down there and personally throw you into the triggerfish tank. That's my policy!"

Kent slammed the phone down and mumbled some obscenities before stretching his neck from the left to right and in a circular motion. He got up from the desk and walked out of his office, down the hallway to the game room.

Two attractive young girls were sitting on his big black couch, and in the far corner sat Moro, his bodyguard. Moro could usually be found lurking close by, not so much to protect Kent but to protect the drugs and money. He was a big Samoan and well versed in martial arts and competent with his Glock-17 pistol.

The game room had a pool table and a dartboard and framed photos of naked girls adorning the walls. The windows had a panoramic view of the San Francisco Bay, and the room was adorned with shag carpeting and leather panels on some of the walls. There was a 100-gallon tank with exotic saltwater fish in the corner and a rosewood cabinet filled with scuba gear. In his younger years, Kent used to scuba dive, and one of his favorite stories was how he had once been confronted by a great white shark and used his WASP diving knife to blow up the shark.

The WASP military knife contains a cylinder of compressed gas in the hilt. When stabbing a subject, about one cubic foot of CO2 gas stored at 800 psi is rapidly injected into the wound, which causes much more damage both from the displacement of internal organs and the freezing effect of the expansion of the gas. One well-placed hit can easily kill or immobilize a large animal. No one knew if his tale of the shark encounter was true, but nevertheless, he proudly displayed the knife on the wall next to the fish tank. He loved his fish, especially the expensive triggerfish.

Kent walked over to a full-size refrigerator and pulled out a pack of Ballpark franks. He slid out one of the franks and broke off a piece and walked over to the fish tank and dropped the piece inside. Four triggerfish attacked it with vigor. He loved watching them devour the meat. In the far corner of the tank, there was a dead triggerfish near the bottom of the tank. He motioned to Moro. "Get rid of the dead one." Moro immediately got up and went over to the cabinet and scooped out the fishnet and went to work. Kent chewed on the frank and threw in a few more chunks for the fish to eat.

Kent had a privileged life in that he inherited most of his money and never had to work too hard. He was a happy guy smoking pot, ordering up hookers, and letting his minions run his businesses, including the sex trafficking. His cell phone rang, and he pulled it out of his fanny pack.

"Yeah! Where've you been? Ok. Yeah, good. Listen to me. You shouldn't have brought the new girl to the party. Her face was all over the news. Next time keep her at the house." Kent kept listening and went over and plopped down between the two girls on the couch. Then he reached into the fanny pack and pulled out a .45 caliber bullet and unscrewed the top of it and poured out a line of cocaine onto his glass table. While listening to the call he snorted the line. "Why did you invite that loser Hitsman to the party?"

On the other end of the call, Gilman gritted his teeth. In truth he had invited him because he was trying to show off and partially because he never felt any of the high school shit he had done to him was significant. "Don't worry about him. He knows the deal and he ain't going to squeal. I just thought he might appreciate our operation and the talent. His arm candy was quite the looker."

"If he rats us out it's on you and you'll have to take care of it."

"He never ratted us out in high school. Don't worry about it."

"True. He's still a pussy. Okay. When is the next shipment?" asked Kent.

"Next week. I'll be heading down to meet them. It's a larger than usual shipment."

"Have you heard from Paul?"

"No. I was going to give him a call."

"Have him call me."

"Will do, Boss."

Kent tossed his phone back into his fanny pack and leaned back into the leather couch. "Okay, who wants to suck my dick?"

The girls giggled nervously.

Boondocks

Boondocks was rummaging through trash containers behind a warehouse hoping to find some old canvas tarps or pieces of carpeting or some other dirty decorative trash he could make use of and bring back to his homeless encampment. And if he happened to find a bottle of Jack Daniels with a couple of swigs left, even better. He tossed out a couple of steel rods onto a pile of growing debris next to the container. *I could reinforce my tent with these beauties*, he thought to himself. He hauled himself up, and with great effort climbed out of the garbage container and slid down onto the pavement. Suddenly a spotlight lit him up as he was getting to his feet. Boondocks covered his eyes with his hand and cursed as two police officers exited a patrol car and approached him.

"Hands! Let me see both your hands." Boondocks raised both hands as best he could while continuing to shield his eyes. Officer Chuck "The Chucker" Evans, a thirteen-year veteran with a Dwayne Johnson physique looked at the pile of debris next to the garbage container and the already partially filled grocery cart. "What's your name?"

"They call me Boondocks."

"Boondocks, do you have any weapons on you, any knives or anything else?"

"No, no, no. Uh, just looking for recycles." Under his breath but a bit too loud he finished the sentence with, "You stupid pigfucker."

He was airborne immediately. He crashed into the side of the warehouse. Officer Chuck Evans had earned his nickname "The Chucker" not because it was a play on his name but because if you gave him any attitude on the street he would pick you up and chuck you through the air into the nearest wall. Boondocks was now experiencing this firsthand as he bounced off the concrete wall and crumpled to the ground in a urine-soaked splat. Boondocks groaned and shook his head to get rid of the stars he was seeing.

"You just got chucked." The officers looked at each other with a slight grin. "Now let's try this again, Boondocks."

"Hey, Partner. Open door." Officer Jerry Chew caught Evans' attention. A few feet to the left from where they were standing Officer Chew shined his Streamlight on a door that was ajar and leading to the interior of the warehouse.

"Boondocks, were you in the warehouse?"

Breathless from his encounter with the wall, Boondocks slowly stuttered, "No, I swear. I didn't even see it was open."

"Are you sure? I better not find any valuables from the warehouse in your cart."

"No, Brother, I swear. I was just in them two trash bins."

"Call it in," Evans said to Chew.

Chew keyed his mic which was pinned to the front part of his uniform shirt. "Headquarters, Paul 138."

"Go ahead 138," came the crackly dispatcher's voice over the radio.

"We're 10-97 on an open door at a warehouse behind Markham Lumber. I'll get you the exact address in a minute."

"10-4, 138. Do you need a cover unit?"

Before Chew could answer, Evans responded on his radio, "Negative, we'll advise." Then he turned back to Boondocks. "Don't go anywhere, because if I have to come find you I'm going to stuff everything in that grocery cart down your throat."

Boondocks gave him a sloppy hand salute and then just continued to lay on the ground sucking air and holding his ribs.

Evans led the way as he slowly pushed the door open and shined his light into the darkness. Guns drawn and Streamlights in hand, they entered the warehouse one by one, Evans going to his right and Chew to his left. They passed some large shelves, but for the most part it was a giant vacant space.

Then in the middle of the space, something caught their eye. They both reacted simultaneously and shined their lights on it. Slowly, they approached with their Streamlights and guns aimed at the object. As they got closer, they glanced at each other silently confirming they were both indeed seeing the same thing.

Evans angled to get in front of the object then grimaced as he realized what he was looking at. Transfixed in two beams of lights from the officers Streamlights was a bloated, naked man tied to a chair. He looked like he was made of pewter with a grey powder tint all over his face and body. Chew shined his light down and saw a fire extinguisher at the man's feet with masking tape on the nozzle fitted around the dead man's mouth. A second fire extinguisher was resting a few feet from them.

"Holy shit!"

Both Chew and Evans quickly spun around in the direction of the voice and saw Boondocks standing behind them, mouth agape, staring past them at the dead man.

The Chair Statue

Detective Hawthorne stooped down to have a closer look at the dead body tied to the chair. He made sure to stay out of the way of the crime scene photographer snapping photos of the fire extinguishers and various angles of the body.

Natalie Martinez lifted the crime scene tape behind Detective Hawthorne and sidled up next to him. "Do you think that's Paul Clark?" she asked.

"It's hard to tell with all that crap on him. We'll have to wait till the medical examiner makes a positive ID."

"Hey, detectives! We've got something here!"

Dolan Harris, one of the crime scene technicians, was pointing to the left foot of the body.

Hawthorne stood up and put his notebook in his coat pocket and walked over to where the tech was kneeling and pointing. Sticking out from underneath the arch of the left foot was some kind of object. It looked like a note or card or something similar.

"You snapped a photo?"

Dolan nodded in the affirmative, so Hawthorne put on a glove and reached down and gently pulled out the object and blew the grey powder off. He showed it to Martinez who was standing behind him.

"Well, I guess we don't need to wait for confirmation from the medical examiner."

"No, I guess we won't."

Hawthorne was holding Paul Clark's driver's license.

Natalie shivered. "What do you make of this?"

"It was personal. I think someone went to a lot of trouble to do this and didn't care about cleaning up and wanted us to know it was Paul Clark. I'm also guessing we're going to come up empty when we follow the paper trail on who last rented this facility."

"What do you mean?" she asked.

"This was a pretty bold killing. I'm sure they covered their tracks. Most likely used a shell company to rent the place. There was no sign of forced entry. We'll find out. One step at a time."

Natalie sighed. "I'll start digging deeper into his past. Maybe he gave someone a wrong prescription and there were some adverse reactions and this was payback."

"Or maybe he just pissed off the wrong person. Whoever did this…he enjoyed it."

****

Kent walked out the front door of his house with Moro following close behind him. Kent stopped halfway up the walkway and turned to Moro. He was gesticulating wildly, and Moro appeared to be arguing back. Moro finally threw his hands up and turned away and Kent continued up his walkway and then walked over to his Humvee and got in it and pulled out of the driveway. All this was observed through the lens of a camera. *So, Kent didn't always have his bodyguard with him*, Tom thought. *This is good to know.*

Kent was followed and photographed for the next three days. Sometimes Moro went with him, sometimes Kent was solo. The key would be catching him when he was solo. The big guy could be a major problem. Tom did his best *Rockford Files* following technique in trying to not get spotted as he followed Kent on some mundane errands like going to an exotic fish store then to a fish-n-chips restaurant where he ate lunch, then to a scuba shop. There seemed to be a theme going on this particular day, but the important part was that Kent was not concerned with his surroundings unless it was a hot girl. Nabbing the little moron would not be too difficult when he was alone.

****

Natalie hopped out of her Lexus with her dry cleaning and briskly walked about a half-block down past storefronts and into the dry cleaners where she had been going for the past year. The neighborhood had slowly been changing, and in the last six months, she sensed it was rougher. She lived on the outskirts of Korea Town because the rents were a bit lower there and she liked the people and the food. When she came out of the dry cleaner, she walked back to her car while reading text messages on her cell. She looked up as she got to her car and found a young Black man leaning against the hood of her car. He was dressed in wannabe gang-banger attire complete with shades and bandana. His crew of four were loitering a few feet away.

Natalie stopped short of him and looked him up and down. "Get off my car."

He chuckled. "What do I get if I get off yo' car, pretty mama?"

"You get to walk away in one piece."

Collective "ooohs" came from his crew as they snickered and jived. He looked over at them then back at her. "Maybe you don't know who you're talking to, but you best take a less aggressive stance and maybe," he winked at his crew, "this will be your lucky day."

"Actually, I do know who I am talking to. Someone who is about to have a very unlucky day." Natalie pulled her coat to her side and exposed her badge on her belt. At this his crew shucked and jived, laughing and enjoying the show.

"Well, well, well. Lady cop. Whatcha gonna do? Arrest me for leaning on your car?" He grinned.

Natalie walked up to him and looked him in the eyes that were hiding behind the sunglasses. "No. I'm not going to arrest you. I'm going to kick your balls up into your throat, break your nose with my elbow, sweep your feet out from under you, and then I'm going to stand on your head and pose for a photo op with your crew."

His crew went nuts at this and were hopping up and down, hooting and hollering. His grin faded and he straightened up off the car, his jaw clenched as he sized her up. Then he relaxed and smiled. "I like you. You are hot-blooded." He side-stepped away from her, making sure he didn't make any contact with her. "Till we meet again."

Natalie watched him stroll with a bounce in his step back to his crew and then went to the driver's side and got in her car. She saw the man slap one of his buddies in the back of the head as they laughed at him, and he cursed a few choice words at them. Yes, the neighborhood was changing.

Spa Day

Tom Hitsman was elated. It was finally spa day, and he had Kent Lim right where he wanted him. It had taken a lot of planning and three days of watching Kent's moves so he could take him without getting caught. Now, here Kent sat in his underwear, on the blades of a forklift about four feet off the ground. He was tied up to the front of the forklift and had also been injected with ketamine during the abduction. Ketamine is an anesthetic used by veterinarians, but it can also be effective on humans but for a shorter window of time. The effects are similar to paralysis.

Tom splashed water on Kent's face to speed up his recovery. Kent's head wobbled as he regained consciousness. He mumbled, but the black masking tape across his mouth muffled him.

"Hey, there. Look who's awake. Hi, Kent. How's it hanging?" Kent's eyes tried to focus. "That was quite a party you threw after the reunion. I have to say, you've really upped your game. From selling *Playboy* magazines in high school to eager freshmen to selling underaged girls to politicians and celebrities. That's quite a feat. I'm surprised you've been able to keep this going as long as you have without getting caught. I attribute that to your partners, Gilman and Clark. Speaking of which, did you hear about Clark? He's dead. He sucked on a fire extinguisher and overdosed. I don't mean fire extinguisher as a euphemism for a bong. I mean an actual fire extinguisher."

Kent tried to focus again but his head felt heavy and wobbly.

"All right, let's cut to the chase. Today is spa day." Kent's head started to droop down. The hitman slapped him across the face. "Oh no. Stay awake, Kent. Look at me. Don't be passing out. I don't want to have to give you an adrenaline shot. That would make your heartbeat too fast, which would lead to you bleeding out. It would ruin the day. LOOK AT ME! I'm going to kill your fish!"

Suddenly Kent looked wide awake. He started looking at his surroundings and understanding his dire situation.

Tom chuckled. "Gilman was right. You really love your fish, don't you? I'm just kidding. Your fish are safe. Ok, now that I have your full attention…. Back in high school, you were a privileged little asswipe. I'm not going to go into details because we both know what you did and I already shot my load talking about it with Clark. If you're thinking of bribing your way out—well, I have money so you're shit out of luck. So, let's get back to spa day. Since you like being pampered and have been all your life, I think you're really going to enjoy this.

"We are going to start out with an activity I'm sure you are familiar with because it's a big tourist attraction in Korea and Indonesian countries. Did you know in Seoul you can walk into a hip café and drink your coffee and then treat yourself to a fish pedicure? You know what I'm talking about? You put your feet into a big tub of water and all these little fish called the Garra Rufa nibble away at the dead skin on your feet. I've seen videos on YouTube and it looks like it tickles. Well, come to find out, the Garra Rufa is not legal in the United States because they could pose a threat to native plant and animal life if released into the wild, so they are not that easy to come by.

"Oh, and here's another interesting fact. Did you know they starve the fish, which is why they eat the skin off the feet? Kind of inhumane if you ask me, starving those poor fish and forcing them to eat the dead skin off of stupid tourists' feet. You would never starve your fish, would you?"

Kent looked down at his bare feet. They were dangling above a ten-by-ten metallic tub of water.

"I ordered some of the Garra Rufa from overseas, and I'll be damned if they didn't send the wrong fucking fish. You know what they sent me? Take a guess."

Kent mumbled weakly underneath his gag.

Tom smiled. "They sent me piranhas. Can you believe that? And boy it was not easy getting them in that tank there. They haven't eaten in about a week, cause it's not like you can walk into Petco and ask them for piranha food. Throw in two weeks in transit and that's probably closer to three weeks of no food for these poor piranhas. Anyway, I really wanted to start out your spa day with a nice pedicure, but this will have to do. Don't worry, I won't let them eat too much. We still have more activities planned."

Tom jumped up onto the forklift and turned on the motor, the diesel engine sputtering and coming to life. Kent struggled on the forklift blades and tried to lift his feet as far up as he could.

"Ok, going down." Tom pulled a lever on the forklift and the blades started lowering Kent into the tank. He lowered him slowly until his feet were submerged and the water became a flurry of waves. The water turned blood red as muffled screams emanated from behind Kent's taped mouth.

"Damn. You got a set of lungs on you for being a little squirt." Tom leaned over the front of the forklift so he could view the action. "Oh, man, that is a gnarly pedicure you're getting there."

Kent continued to scream, his face becoming as red as the water. Suddenly, his head fell forward as he passed out.

"Man, what a pansy." Tom pulled back the lever on the forklift and lifted Kent out of the water, his feet ravaged, flesh ripped away, exposing bone. Tom maneuvered the forklift across the warehouse, leaving a trail of blood in his wake.

An hour later, when Kent woke, he was lying on his back in a bed with white silk sheets. He raised his head and tried to look around.

Tom rushed to his side. "Easy there, buddy. Don't strain your neck." He pushed a pillow underneath Kent's head. "Lay back, relax." Tom adjusted the pillow. "Are you comfortable?"

Kent winced in pain and looked toward his feet. The silk sheets were covering his feet, but there were blotches of red seeping through the sheets.

"Yeah, your feet are not in the best of shape. I bandaged them up the best I could and gave you a little morphine for the pain. It's probably wearing off."

Kent tried to move, then realized his hands and arms were tied to the bedpost. He tried to speak. Tom yanked the tape off his mouth and Kent squealed. In a ragged voice, Kent spit out the first thing that came to mind. "Fuck you, you fucking loser."

Tom's jaw dropped momentarily before he erupted into laughter. "You really don't understand the concept of leverage, do you? Let me educate you since you obviously learned nothing in high school. I am your captor, you are my prisoner. I hold all the cards, you hold absolutely nothing. Not even your dick in your hand. You are the ball, I am the bat. I am the windshield, you are the bug. I decide if you live or die and how painful that death will be. You see how that works? I have what some people would refer to as leverage over you, and yet you insult me. You see how that doesn't work in your favor?"

Kent tugged on his restraints and spit at Tom, barely missing him.

"Wow. You are one stupid fuck." Tom ripped off a piece of duct tape from a roll and slapped it over Kent's mouth. "Look above you."

For the first time, Kent looked above him and saw a big circular black object that looked like one of the big magnets they use at a wrecking yard to pick up vehicles and move them around.

"That there is a machine used to test the firmness of urethane foams including car seats, furniture, mattresses, bedding, pillows, foam products, and materials, and bolsters. It presses down and compresses the material, going deeper each time. Of course, there are different compression settings and a timer, and I have modified it for top compression. You are lying on a $1,000 mattress that I was thinking of buying for myself, but first I want to test it. At first, this may be annoying, but in a few hours, you'll be begging me to kill you. Which I won't. I'm going to get some lunch and you should try and get some sleep. If you can."

Tom walked to the side of the machine and pushed a button and turned it on. The giant circular disc slowly moved down on top of Kent, the circumference of the disc covering most of his upper torso. It slowly depressed Kent into the mattress about an inch and then retracted. Kent's face was red again as he struggled against the restraints. The machine started back down again and made contact with his pudgy body and depressed him again into the mattress about an inch.

"I'll be back in a couple of hours. That's a pretty sturdy mattress, so it should hold up pretty well. Which, unfortunately, may not work in your favor. Leverage, Kent. It's all about leverage. Oh, and one more thing. I know you're a fan of music, so I picked a song that I think is appropriate for this monumental event."

Tom aimed the remote controller at a boom box and blasted "I'm a Steamroller, Baby, I'm Gonna Roll all Over You." It was a blues song originally written and recorded by James Taylor, but this was the Elvis Presley rendition from the 70s. The steady blues-style thumping bass and drums kept the rhythm going and Elvis rocked his voice on top of the music. "I'm a steam roller baby, Yeah, I'm gonna roll all over you."

Tom exited the warehouse through a side door, and for a moment Kent saw a slice of light shine in from outside. Then his entire body felt the weight of the machine as it crushed him into the mattress once again and darkness closed in on him.

Fish-n-Chips

Tom had just finished ordering his fish-n-chips when his cell phone vibrated. He looked at the number and reluctantly answered.

"Where are you?"

"I'm not your damn dog sitter. I said I'd watch him for a couple of days and it's been a week."

Tom grimaced at the sound of the voice as he grabbed his tray and meal. "I'll be home tomorrow night. How's he doing?" Tom pulled the phone away from his ear anticipating the verbal diatribe.

"He's fine. He ate one of my shoes." There was a pause on the other end and then the voice said, "I miss you, baby. Looking forward to seeing you." The voice was now sweet.

Amy was back in town and was cozying up to Tom again.

After her relentless nagging about the incident in San Francisco, Tom finally admitted to her that he was working on a plan to take them down. It was against his better instinct, but even Samson had his weakness when it came to Delilah. Tom didn't go into detail, but he told Amy he may need her help at some point. This seemed to placate her, and she got very excited about the prospect of taking these creeps down. Tom explained that he would tell her when the time was right, but the less she knew the better off she would be if anything went wrong.

"I miss you too."

"Does your trip have anything to do with, well, you know…." asked Amy.

Tom gritted his teeth. It probably was a bad idea to tell her anything. Look at what happened to Samson. "I have to get going, but, yes. I'll see you soon," Tom responded, irritated, before ending the call. He knew the likelihood of anyone listening in on the call was slim to none, but he didn't want to take any chances. He had worked too hard to let this go awry and come back to haunt him.

Tom finished his fish-n-chips and decided to stop by a park he had seen along the way before getting back to Kent. He walked past the sandbox where kids were playing with moms watching and picked a bench facing the sun. He sat and extended his arms along the top of the bench and closed his eyes, letting the warmth of the sun wash over him. He could feel the sun penetrating every pore on his face and hands. It felt different today. He felt different. He felt alive. His senses were heightened.

Manicures and Murder

Dale Hawthorne walked down the hallway toward the detective bureau. He walked past a man handcuffed to a bench looking like he was going to throw up. The man made eye contact with him for a second before quickly casting his eyes down. Hawthorne entered the detective bureau and walked over to his desk. Detective Mark Jacobsen was sitting at the desk across from him filling out some paperwork.

"Was that Steve De Soto the city councilman I saw hooked up to the bench?"

"Yeah," said Jacobsen.

"Or should I say the soon-to-be-former city councilman?"

"Oh yeah?" asked Hawthorne.

"He was caught snapping 'up-the-skirt' photos of a fourteen-year-old girl at the Target on Westgate. And get this. When they searched him, they found a map of different stores in the area and which days they waxed the floors."

"I don't get it?" said a perplexed Hawthorne.

"He was photographing up the skirt by shooting the reflection off the floor, so he needs shiny floors."

Hawthorne took a moment to let it sink in. "Damn. That's a whole new level of pervert. Who caught him?"

"The kid's mom caught him and confronted him and he made a run for it, so she chased him screaming bloody murder. Luckily a security guard tackled him just before he got out into the parking lot. When the uniforms got there, they reviewed the in-store surveillance video which was enough for them to hook him up. The video showed him snapping photos of the floor, but then he held the phone right under the girl's skirt and that's when the mom saw him. They recovered his cell phone but they can't unlock it and he ain't saying shit. Just asked for his lawyer."

"What's the chief saying?" asked Hawthorne.

"The chief didn't want him in a holding cell until we know for sure what's on the phone, but either way, I don't think this bodes well for him. Fucking pervert."

Hawthorne shook his head. "Never ceases to amaze me."

The sound of heels clicking on the floor alerted Hawthorne that Martinez was walking into the bureau.

Jacobson got up from his desk. “Well, I better go tell the councilman that unless he cooperates with us he’s going to be the new nut-nuzzling fuck-puppet at county jail.” He smiled lasciviously at Martinez as he walked past her and out of the bureau.

Martinez ignored him and walked straight over to Hawthorne and placed a file folder on his desk. “I was going through Paul Clark’s finances. He is really well off for being a pharmacist. I mean millionaire well off, which got me curious, so I dug a little deeper. It turns out he’s a partner in a side business that brings in a lot of the revenue. KNLM International. It’s a string of nail salons operating in California. Seventeen to be exact.”

“What’s he doing with a nail salon business? Seems out of left field.”

“I thought so too, so I looked into it and called his wife. Apparently, it’s an old high school buddy of his who owns them. He got involved with him about fifteen years ago. She’s not really sure what his role is, but it has to do with the finances of the business. Apparently, Clark was majoring in accounting before he switched to the pharmaceutical field.”

“Can nail salons generate that kind of income?” asked Hawthorne.

"Well, that's what I am looking into. But that's not the interesting part. When I followed the lead, I found that KNLM is owned by Kent Lim. He's Korean and not Vietnamese, which is odd since most of those salons are Vietnamese-owned and operated. But here's the kicker. I tried to contact Lim to get a read on him and see what kind of reaction he would have to Clark's death, just in case there was a falling out between them, and turns out he didn't have any reaction at all…because he's dead."

"What?" Hawthorne looked up from his computer.

"He was murdered two days ago in San Francisco. The local PD is sending me more info, but apparently it was a very elaborate murder. The dick handling the case actually used the word 'genius' if you can believe that."

"What do you mean?" asked Hawthorne.

"He was tortured. First, he was dipped into a pool of piranhas that ate his feet, and then the perp rigged up some kind of gizmo that crushed him to death in a bed."

"Jesus." Hawthorne pondered the obvious.

Then Martinez asked the obvious. "Are you thinking what I'm thinking?"

Hawthorne ran his hand through his thick dark hair. "Well, it's hard not to. There's definitely a connection between the victims, and both were very personal kills. Did you tell them about Clark?"

"No, it didn't come up."

"Good. Let's keep it like that for now. Let's see what they send us, and with any luck maybe we'll find a connection in the scene evidence. Then we'll know for sure. I think we should start looking at the company organization. Find out who's been fired or who had an ax to grind. Nothing is really above board in that kind of business, and the fact that you even found a paper trail is rare. Was he the only other partner?"

"I haven't dug that deep yet. Why?"

"Like I said before, this was personal and carried out by someone who also had access to funds, so maybe there was a third silent partner. And like you said, maybe there was a falling out between them. Good work." Hawthorne sat in his chair and grabbed the files Natalie had brought with her.

Natalie motioned toward the hallway. "Isn't that City Councilman De Soto? Kinda early in the day for getting popped for a DUI."

"Oh, I'm pretty sure a DUI would be looking really good right about now for ol' Steve De Soto."

A perplexed Natalie looked back out toward the hallway and then shrugged, sat at her desk, and started working on her computer.

Hitsman Laments

Tom popped open a can of Arnold Palmer lemonade and sat in front of his computer. He went to the *Baltimore Sun* website and skipped to the crime section and read the current headline "Still No Leads In Gruesome Wearhouse Murder." He clicked on the link and began reading about the gruesome murder of a prominent pharmacist and how he had been tortured and killed with a fire extinguisher. The police were calling it a crime of passion and were looking into all known associates. The article gave out some details but not all. He figured the cops were holding back some evidence in case they got a suspect, and also as a way to weed out all the wackos that would be calling in to take responsibility. It was strange how whenever there was a sensational murder random people would step up and claim responsibility for heinous crimes they didn't commit. Hard to know if they just wanted the fifteen minutes of fame or were truly psychos.

After reading the article, Tom was fairly certain he had covered his tracks effectively. However, he would keep tabs on it and watch his back. He then surfed to the *San Francisco Examiner* and once again went to the crime beat section. He found a small entry that said, "Man Killed In Gang War." There were no details of the killing other than the location. The name was withheld, and it was still an active case. *That is odd*, Tom thought to himself. He was hoping that the details of how he had killed Kent would be all over the Internet. It was a pretty genius way to kill someone after all. Tom was sure he had covered his tracks, and he went over the details in his mind.

He flashed back on that wonderful day. When he had returned to the warehouse after eating his fish-n-chips, he was surprised to find that Kent was a bloody soggy spot on the mattress. The giant machine had crushed him to death. Tom guessed he hadn't calibrated it correctly, and he was disappointed that he wasn't there for Kent's last breath, but also because he had one more pampering treatment for Kent. He was going to put him into a self-tanning booth and let him cook to death. Oh well. This killing stuff was still new to Tom, and he couldn't expect to get it down perfectly the first couple of times. He was lucky that he had been able to catch Kent alone without his bodyguard. He figured his bodyguard would end up getting the rath from Gilman.

That fucker Gilman. He was going to be tricky to catch since he was going to be on alert once he found out Kent and Clark were dead. Plus, he was a big imposing guy and a psychotic asshole. Rather than take him straight on, Tom decided he would find him the way his other customers did. He searched his desk for the business card Gilman had given him at the reunion.

The Dark Web

After about an hour of searching various forums, Tom got a ping back from an anonymous source. He had been inquiring about Darren Gilman. The anonymous source said one word: *Cadizig1*.

This was interesting. Tom had been inquiring under the pretense of wanting to do some business with Gilman but had lost contact with him. Pretty lame, he thought, and wasn't expecting any response so he was taken aback when he got the message. *Cadizig1*. What did that mean? On a whim, Tom did a Google search on Cadizig1 and got a hit. It was a forum for Cadillac enthusiasts where someone had created a profile with the name of Cadizig1. However, when he clicked on it the profile came back empty. He then hacked into the California Department of Motor Vehicles database and found an automobile registered to Gilman, but after following up on the address listed he found it was a P.O. box at a strip mall in Simi Valley. The vehicle registered to him was a Cadillac SUV.

So, Gilman liked Cadillacs, but he kept his identity under the radar. He went back to the dark web and went to a forum he was familiar with and left a message for him.

Cadizig1 - I understand you might be able to help me out on a transaction. I'm looking for something special. Please let me know next steps - Terminal Hitman

He signed it with his handle, *Terminal Hitman.* He knew that was a very cocky move as Gilman might know who was contacting him, but why not. Let's play. With the right planning, Tom would dispose of him—in a very ingenious way, of course. Nothing but the best for Gilman.

Tom pushed back from his desk and grabbed a new miniature tennis ball for his dog. Marty loved playing with those little tennis balls, but he only liked the smell of new balls, and after about fifteen minutes he would lose interest. So, Tom was constantly going to the pet store and buying him new balls. Yes, he spoiled the dog, but it's a dog's life. It made the dog happy and that made Tom happy. Killing Gilman would make him even happier. Marty growled in the background as he whipped the ball around and then chased it.

Lights go Down in the City

Gilman was sitting in his SUV Cadillac down the street from Kent's San Francisco flat. After Moro called him to tell him Kent was dead and that the police were there, Gilman had driven to San Francisco overnight. Kent's flat overlooked the San Francisco Bay and was on the outskirts of Twin Peaks. It was a million-dollar view with the Bay Bridge and Treasure Island in view and all of Market Street and the financial center buzzing in the sunlight.

Gilman made sure there were no more cops around and then got out of his SUV and walked toward the residence. He walked up the concrete pathway, past Kent's custom Hummer. He always thought it was comical how a man of small stature would compensate by driving a Hummer. Kent could barely see over the dash when he drove that thing, but he was extremely proud of it. Now that Kent was gone maybe he would add the Hummer to his collection. Gilman entered the security code and the front door buzzed and clicked. He pushed the door open and walked inside, through the hallway passing a couple of bedrooms, turned left and walked past the kitchen, and found Moro in the game room smoking pot.

"What the fuck happened?" demanded Gilman as he walked in.

Moro exhaled a cloud of smoke. "Bro, someone killed the boss. Fucked him up good."

"Well, where the fuck were you? Why weren't you with him?"

"You know Kent. Sometimes he just takes off and doesn't tell me. I'm not his shadow. He pays me to protect his shit here."

Gilman looked around and out the window at the beautiful view. He shook his head. "Yeah, I do know Kent. What did the cops say?"

"You know they were making like I had something to do with it. I told them I hadn't seen him in a couple of days. I got fucked up on some new ganja and was playing video games with Tiana. They checked the security video and confirmed I've been here."

"What else did they say?"

"They said piranhas ate his feet."

Gilman grimaced slightly and looked over at the giant fish tank where Kent had his triggerfish.

"And then he was crushed to death. In a bed," continued Moro.

"He was crushed in a bed?"

"Yeah. Five-O were pretty impressed too. Said it was well planned out. Someone probably had a grudge. Asked me if I knew who hated Kent. I said, 'everyone.'" Moro laughed. "And one more thing. Paul's wife called. He's dead too."

Gilman was speechless for a moment. "Paul is dead?"

"Ya, bro. He was killed too. His wife wanted to know if Kent had anything to do with it"

Gilman was silent. He turned away from Moro and stared out at the glistening San Francisco Bay and the container ships dotting the blue water. After a minute of grinding his jaw, he turned back to Moro. "Did you tell the cops about Paul?"

"No, bro. What's going on?"

"I'm not sure. But I am sure the cops are going to start digging, and that is not good. They will eventually connect the dots."

"What do I tell the cops if they come back?"

"Nothing. Don't let them take anything unless they have a search warrant. Right now, we need to clean this place of anything that points to our 'other business.' *And me*, he thought to himself. "I can see someone wanting to whack Kent. He probably deserved it. But Paul?" Gilman thought for a moment and then marched down the hallway to Kent's office. Moro followed closely. Gilman sat at Kent's mahogany desk and then opened the laptop and turned it on. "Do you know his password?" he asked Moro.

"No, bro. But he keeps them taped to the bottom of the desk there."

Gilman reached under the desk and found a notepad taped to the underside. He yanked it off and looked at it. There were passwords with dates. The latest one was changed two weeks ago. It was *!suckmeoff22bitch*.

Gilman shook his head then entered the password. The computer came to life and Gilman opened Chrome and did a search for Paul Clark. After scrolling down the page, he found the news report from the *Boston Globe*. He clicked on the link and read the article. When he was done, he gritted his teeth and his breathing became more noticeable. He closed the lid to the computer. "Did that little asshole Kent try and expand into someone else's territory without telling me?"

Moro shrugged. "No, bro. He always lets you handle that part of the business. You know that."

"This isn't some random killing. These guys had a vendetta. They killed Paul by making him inhale an entire fire extinguisher."

Moro made a face. "Damn Bro. What do you want to do?"

"We have to find a new safehouse for the girls. Whoever did this may make a move on the merchandise next."

Day Tripper

Hawthorne sat in Captain Joe Kelly's office. The captain listened intently as Hawthorne laid out what he had discovered in his investigation of the Clark killing. Captain Joe was one of the likable members of the brass at the department. He was affable and gave accolades to his men when deserved. He didn't believe that you had to be a stone-faced asshole to be a good commanding officer and felt he got more respect from his troops than some of his counterparts who were all by the book and had the personality of a mallet.

Hawthorne finished his brief and said, "So, what do you think?"

"I think you're right," said Captain Kelly. "Definitely a connection. Have you had a video conference with the SFPD detectives yet?"

"I thought it would be better if I had an in-person meeting and had a look at the crime scene myself."

"Wait a minute. That's what this is about? You're trying to get a free trip to California!"

Hawthorne couldn't help but laugh knowing his ruse was up. "Well, I don't think they are going to want to come out to Baltimore!"

The captain shook his head and chuckled while leaning back in his chair. "Why can't you just do a video thingamajig like everyone else."

"You mean a Zoom meeting?" asked Hawthorne.

"A what?" replied the captain.

"Case in point," countered Hawthorne.

Captain Kelly blew out a breath. "Okay. But no Top of the Mark. Three days."

Hawthorne stood up. "Thanks, Cap. What about Martinez?"

"Martinez stays here."

"She's gonna claim discrimination," countered Hawthorne.

"Martinez stays here. Now get out of here before I change my mind."

Hawthorne got up from the chair and started for the door.

"Oh, one more thing," chimed the captain. "If you get the chance, can you bring back one of those cable car souvenirs? The wife loves the cable cars."

"Sure, Cap. You got it." As an afterthought, the captain yelled out one more instruction at Hawthorne. "And get a connecting flight! We're not made of money!"

Hawthorne shook his head. "It's always about the money."

"Always," retorted Captain Kelly. "Especially when they are trying to defund us," he mumbled under his breath.

Hawthorne walked back to his desk just as his phone rang. "I'll be right there." He walked out of the detective room and down the hall and came to one of the interview rooms where Officer Philips met him.

"Sorry for dragging you into this, but Jacobson is out today."

"No, that's fine. What do you have?"

"You remember we popped City Councilman De Soto for being a pervert? I guess he realized he's in deeper shit than he thought because he's in there with his lawyer. Says he has some info on a sex trafficking ring and wants to make a deal."

Hawthorne nodded. "Alright, thanks."

Hawthorne opened the door and slipped into the room. Seated on the other side of a table was Councilman Steve De Soto and his lawyer, Jack Stanford. De Soto was a skinny, fidgety man with small bug eyes, a receding hairline, and looked to be in his late forties. He sat with his hands folded in front of him, looking down at the table. Hawthorne took a seat across from them. Hawthorne eyed De Soto then turned his gaze to the lawyer. He was familiar with the lawyer from previous encounters that involved high-profile DUI cases.

"Jack, good to see you. What can I do for you?"

"Detective Hawthorne, my client has some information that we feel will be of interest to you. I already spoke with D.A. Ashcroft, and she said she may consider leniency if this information proves to be accurate and useful."

Hawthorne nodded and then looked over at De Soto. "Ok. What sort of information, Steve?"

Steve didn't look up at Hawthorne. He started wringing his hands together, beads of sweat forming on his pasty forehead. "There are these parties." Hawthorne waited. "These social mixers with girls. Young girls." De Soto rubbed and squeezed his hands more intensely.

"And you've been to these parties?" asked Hawthorne.

DeSoto nodded, his voice cracking as he said, "Yes."

"And what happens at these parties?"

De Soto sat still as if in a trance until Jack put his hand on his shoulder, nudging him. "Anything you want," De Soto softly replied.

Hawthorne could see that this was painful for De Soto and that he would have to tread lightly or the pervert might clam up. If he did have information on a sex trafficking operation, he wanted to know. "Ok, so you are paying for the company of these women?"

De Soto started scratching his left wrist harshly. "Yes. It's a membership. They have these 'CherryPop' parties quarterly. You pay your dues and you can join the events. And it also allows you private access to hotels and sometimes your home. I don't use the private access because I'm not local."

"Where do they have the parties?" asked Hawthorne.

"Usually in Hollywood."

Hawthorne looked at him quizzically. "The Hollywood Hotel downtown?"

"No. Hollywood. In Los Angeles."

Hawthorne pursed his lips together and looked over at Jack. "Seriously? You knew this?"

Jack shrugged his shoulders. "Well, can't you pass on the info and see if it pans out?"

Hawthorne scooted the chair he was sitting in and started to get up.

"They also have parties in San Francisco," chimed out De Soto.

Hawthorne stopped. "The same group?"

"Yes. It's run by the same guys."

"Do you know them?"

"I've seen a couple of them. One of them is Korean. I think he owns a bunch of nail salons. I heard him talking one night."

Hawthorne slowly sat back down as De Soto looked up from the table at him. "Go on," said Hawthorne with keen interest.

View from the Ground

Tom had a window seat overlooking the wing of an A380 Airbus on a flight from Los Angeles to San Francisco. He reached up and turned the knob to get a little airflow going and then watched the ground crew loading luggage into the cargo area of the jet. He was wearing brown Ray-Ban sunglasses, a black baseball cap, black windbreaker, dark blue shirt, and blue jeans, trying to remain non-descript and making sure his face wasn't completely visible to the multiple surveillance cameras he passed when going through the airport. He had used the fake IDs again to purchase the airline tickets and get through security.

Tom had finally heard back from Gilman and made arrangements to have a special present delivered to him at his hotel suite in San Francisco. Now he had to get to San Francisco and into the Top of the Mark hotel. As he thought about the different scenarios that might take place in his showdown with Gilman, another passenger stopped in his aisle and hoisted his duffle bag in the overhead bin. As he adjusted the duffle bag in the bin, his sport coat lifted up exposing a law enforcement badge clipped to his belt. Tom noticed this right away.

The man scooted in and took the seat next to Tom. Both men did the customary nod of acknowledgment as Hawthorne reached next to Tom for the seatbelt. He pulled it up and fastened it across his lap. They sat in silence as more passengers worked their way down the middle of the plane until Tom spoke up out of curiosity. "So how do you like being a cop?"

The man looked at him in surprise. "What makes you think I'm a cop?"

A slight smirk played on Tom's face as he turned slightly toward the man. "I saw the badge on your belt."

The man nodded. "Ah, good. For a second there I thought I sat down next to someone I had previously arrested."

They both lightly laughed.

"Oh, no, no. I try to keep my contact with law enforcement down to a minimum. Not even parking tickets."

"That's a good thing. Parking tickets suck," the man said.

They both sat in silence for a few seconds and then Tom spoke up. "So, seriously, I'm curious. What's it like to be a cop? Or in your case, a detective?"

The man looked over at Tom. "That's right. Homicide. Detective Hawthorne," he replied. "You know, I used to say it's just like any other job. It has its good days and it has its bad days." Hawthorne took a beat then continued as he reflected on the question he had heard a thousand times. "The truth is, our bad days are really bad, and there are times when you can't unsee what you've seen or undo what you've done."

"Sounds difficult," said Tom.

"It can be. But there is also satisfaction knowing you can make a difference." Hawthorne wasn't sure why he was opening up to a stranger on a plane, but he kept talking. "When I was a rookie, I was keenly aware of not violating someone's civil rights because they pound that into you at the police academy. But the streets are completely different from the classroom. I remember my FTO noticed my hesitance and said that it takes time to adjust to a new position of power, but that I had to remember one thing."

"What was that?"

"He said that ninety percent of the people that come into contact with the police do so because they have done something to mitigate the encounter. The average citizen does not come into contact with the police. And he was right.

I soon realized that ninety percent of the people I came into contact with had broken the law, and the other 10% were victims."

Tom nodded as he contemplated this. "So, no gray areas? It's just black and white?"

Hawthorne nodded. "It's easier that way. At least for me."

The overhead speaker crackled to life as the cheery flight attendant picked up the mic and went into her memorized welcome and safety speech, and ended by saying the approximate flight time to San Francisco would be a brisk fifty-five minutes.

"Thank God," said Hawthorne. "I've already been flying for over five hours."

Tom looked over at him. "You're not LAPD?"

Hawthorne shook his head. "No. I'm Baltimore PD."

Tom felt his face flush and his heart rate increase and reflexively pulled out the magazine that was tucked to the back of the seat in front of him. The title read: *How to Prevent Your Personal Data from Being Stolen in Cyber Space*. "Baltimore? What brings you out West?"

“I’m working on some leads that might be connected to one of my investigations.”

Tom’s mouth felt dry. He worked to get the words out without sounding nervous. “It must be important if they sent you out here.”

“Well, all my cases are important, but this one.... This one has found its way to the top of my list.”

Tom opened the magazine and held it closer to his face. He could feel his heart thumping like a snare drum and his face felt as if it were on fire.

“What about you?” asked Hawthorne.

“What do you mean?”

“Are you heading to Frisco for pleasure or business?”

Tom sat in silence for a few moments. He could almost hear the blood rushing through his veins. He pursed his lips together searching for saliva in his mouth. “I’m, uh, I'm going to see a specialist my doctor recommended.”

“Nothing too serious I hope?” said Hawthorne.

“I’m terminal,” said Tom just as the jet engines revved up. He looked out the window and watched the tarmac roll by.

Hawthorne was pretty sure he heard him correctly but opted to say nothing. Instead, he leaned his head back and closed his eyes as the rumble of the plane shot them down the runway, and the plane rotated and lifted ever so gently into the sky.

I'll do it My Way

Gilman had contemplated calling Paul's wife to see if he could get some details on what had happened but then thought the better of it. What if the cops had bugged the phone lines? He didn't need to draw attention to himself with so much to do. Besides, he never really liked that smug ass-licking Paul anyway. Paul insisted on keeping financial records to make things look legit, but of course, Gilman had kept some cash off the books. He wasn't as stupid as Paul thought he was, and the proof was that he was still alive and Paul wasn't. He never understood why Kent kept Paul around. Anyone could cook the books.

Gilman thought back to high school when he first met Paul. Paul, who was a smartass kinda guy, had started cozying up to Kent and trying to push Tommy Hitsman and Gilman out of the picture. They were all hanging out by the bleachers during lunch and Paul had made a smartass remark to Gilman and took off running and laughing. Gilman, without missing a beat, reached down to a wooden stake that was marking off an area of the track and ripped it out of the ground with brute force and with lightning-fast precision, flung it like a javelin. The stake flew through the air in a perfect spiral and nailed Paul in the left calf, taking him down like a gazelle. An amazingly lucky shot that surprised everyone, including Gilman. Paul's laughter turned to a loud yelp as he crumpled in the dust of the track grabbing his calf. Everyone in the bleachers laughed their asses off as Gilman marched calmly toward his wounded quarry.

Upon reaching Paul, he picked him up by his belt and shirt and effortlessly flung him into a group of cheerleaders that were practicing their routine. The crowd in the bleachers roared with laughter as the cheerleaders all screamed and dodged Paul, who landed head first onto a pile of pom-poms. At this point the football coach, Roy Montgomery, ran over to the commotion.

"Hey, Gilman! What's going on here?"

"Uh, nothing, Coach. Just watching Clark do his cheerleading routine."

Everyone burst out laughing as Paul emerged from the fray of pom-poms and spit out some pom-pom strands.

"You working on a new routine, Clark?" Coach facetiously said to Paul.

Paul looked over at Gilman, who was glaring at him and replied as best as he could without showing how much pain he was in. "This cheerleading stuff is harder than I thought." He looked over at the cheerleaders and said, "Thanks for letting me try out."

The head cheerleader looked at him in disgust and said, "Fuck off, creep!"

At this everyone including the coach broke out in hysterical laughter. Paul dusted himself off and hobbled away, glancing back at Gilman.

Coach smirked and looked over at Gilman. "Save your tackles for the games."

Gilman nodded. "Sure thing, Coach." He looked over at one of the cheerleaders with a glint in his eye and she smiled demurely back.

Later that week, Paul and Gilman made peace at Kent's urging and began to hang out together. It was around this time that they began to target Tom with their barbs and bully pranks for the remainder of the school year.

Now that Paul and Kent were out of the way, Gilman could run the business the way he wanted to, and it didn't hurt that he was the one who had all the information on the clients and handled the day-to-day business. He also had the respect of the crews that smuggled the girls and shuttled them from place to place. He just had to make sure he wasn't compromised, and he also needed to figure out who had killed Kent and Paul. They would most likely be coming for him next, but their element of surprise was gone. *Let them come*, he thought. He and his guys would welcome them with salvo and fury.

Gilman had checked the dark web on Kent's computer and had engaged with a potential new client who wanted a special treat delivered to one of the fancy San Francisco hotels. Since he was going to stay in town while he and Moro made plans, he figured it couldn't hurt to take on a new client. He was also a bit intrigued by this new potential client. He had conducted business under the handle of *Terminal Hitman.* Could it possibly be that Tom had come around and wanted to sample the goods? *Nah, Tom was still a pussy.* But what if...

Hotel California

The plane docked at the gate, and everyone popped up out of their seats in a rush to retrieve their overhead luggage and get off the metallic tube which had carried them to their destination without incident. Hawthorne got up out of his seat and reached up to grab his carry-on and then made room for Tom. As Tom pulled his bag a small gym bag that was resting on top of his slid off, heading for his face. He turned his head, but it clipped him and his sunglasses flew off his face. He bent down to grab them, but Hawthorne scooped them up first. Tom and Hawthorne stared at each other momentarily and then Tom smiled and said thanks and took them from him and put them back on. They stepped off the plane onto the gateway and were walking up the ramp when Hawthorne looked back at Tom and said, "I hope everything works out for you."

Tom nodded and replied, "You too," as they entered the main terminal area and dodged the people waiting to board the plane.

****

The door clicked and lit up green as Hawthorne swiped his keycard and entered his hotel room. It was compact and tight with a queen bed, located not too far from the SFPD precinct he would be visiting. He had given some thought to the conversation he had with the stranger on the plane. He couldn't imagine what he would do if he was given a terminal diagnosis. He shivered just thinking at this horrible prospect. As he was unpacking, his cell phone rang and he saw it was Natalie.

"Hey, I was going to call you. Just checked in. Anything new?"

"Yeah. I had another talk with Paul's wife, and she remembered that he was supposed to attend a high school reunion there in the Bay Area. She said she never liked Kent and thinks he might have had something to do with Paul's death."

"When was the reunion?" asked Hawthorne.

"Three months ago."

"Do you have the name of the high school?"

"Yeah. I'll text it to you. They said you can swing by and pick up a list of the people who attended. They also have some video of the gathering. I'll text you the details."

"Ok. I'll meet with SFPD in the morning and then swing by the school in the afternoon." He clicked off and then opened his suitcase and pulled out swim trunks. He was in California after all, so why not enjoy San Francisco's legendary chilly summer weather. He changed into a robe that was hanging in the closet and then headed out the door in search of the pool, only to find that it was closed for renovations. Then he realized he had not slipped the hotel key card into his robe pocket but had left it on the night table inside the room. He thought the only logical thing one thinks at a moment like this: *Fuck me.*

Across town at the Fairmont Hotel, Tom put his duffle bag onto the bed and then took his computer bag over to the desk. He wanted to do some research on Detective Hawthorne. Perhaps he could learn a little more about the investigation in Baltimore. He fired up the laptop and signed into the local wifi. There was a ding on his computer alerting him that there was a new message in the bulletin board he had used to make contact with Gilman. *Are you still interested in receiving your gift?* It was signed *Cadizig1*.

Tom responded and gave him the room number of the hotel suite and confirmed the time. He had already paid a hefty deposit and would pay the balance afterward, and had given Gilman enough of a background that he would be taken seriously but not blackmailed. Of course, all the information he gave Gilman was false, but it would hold up under scrutiny if Gilman decided to try and check him out. His phone vibrated and he looked down and saw that it was Amy. He had been waiting for this phone call.

Picking up the Trail

The giant circular device covered most of the torso, the body crushed and broken, white sheets tainted with dried blood. The arms were restrained, and it looked like they may have been pulled out of the shoulder socket as they did not give way when his body was crushed further and further into the mattress. It was a grisly scene.

Hawthorne slid the photo he had been viewing to the side and looked at the next photo of the crime scene where Kent had been murdered. Hawthorne was sitting in the SFPD Detective Bureau. They in turn were looking at Paul Clark's crime scene photos that Hawthorne had provided. The detective was shaking his head as he reviewed the photos.

"I think you're right. These cases may be related. We were looking at it as a one-off, but this changes things. Do you have any leads?"

Hawthorne decided to hold back on the new information he had on the reunion. "I was hoping you did."

"C'mon, you didn't fly all the way out here just to show us these photos," countered the SF detective.

"What can I say, I love the cable cars."

Introducing Lin

There was a knock on the door and Tom got up from his chair and walked across the suite and looked through a peephole on the door. The fisheye peephole distorted Moro and made him look even bigger than normal, which concerned Tom for a moment. He was expecting Gilman, not a giant Samoan.

Tom opened the door and Moro stood motionless at the entry. Tom motioned him in, and Moro crossed the entry and kept on walking right past Tom and began inspecting the suite. He first checked the living room area and then walked into the bedroom and looked around, opened the closet door, and then came back into the living room and went behind the wet bar and opened some of the drawers and cabinets. Seemingly satisfied, he approached Tom and motioned for him to raise his arms so he could search him.

"Seriously? Is this really necessary?"

Moro didn't answer and instead began patting him down. He was most likely looking for a wire or some kind of recording device. It didn't seem like he was patting him down for weapons. Satisfied, Moro stepped back and said, "The rest of the money."

"Where's my gift?" asked Tom.

"Money first," responded Moro.

"Look, I need to at least see the girl if you expect me to hand over more money. If not, you can get the hell out."

Moro glared at him for a long moment. Tom wasn't sure what to expect. He would either end up with the girl or prone on the floor after receiving a thunderous blow from Moro's cannonball-sized fist. Moro reached into his pocket and pulled out a cell phone. He aimed it at Tom and snapped a photo.

"Hey, what are you doing!"

"Just a little insurance, bro," said Moro.

"That doesn't prove anything other than I am standing in a hotel room," snapped Tom.

Moro ignored him and then started working on a text. He sent a text, put the phone away, and both men waited. What seemed like an eternity passed when there was a light knock on the door. Moro motioned for Tom to go take a look. Tom walked over to the door and looked through the peephole. He saw a man holding the arm of a young woman.

"Money," said Moro.

Tom walked over to Moro and handed him a small envelope he had in his back pocket. Moro opened, looked inside, and thumbed through the bills. He put the envelope into his coat pocket and then walked over, opened the door, and let the man and young girl inside. The Asian man walked with a limp and held the girl tightly by the arm. He walked her over to the couch, and in Vietnamese, told her to sit down. She complied, and then Moro looked at Tom and said in a dead-serious tone, "Two hours." Both men then left.

Tom looked the girl over. She sat very still, but he could see that she was trembling. She had long brown hair, almond skin, and a pretty face. She was wearing a black blouse, blue jean jacket, and tight black spandex pants. He came up to her then sat in the chair across from her and folded his hands in front of him. She definitely looked like the young girl that had gone missing four months ago. What she had been through, he couldn't imagine.

"Would you like some water?" asked Tom. The girl shook her head no without looking at him. Tom got up off the ornate chair and the girl instinctively flinched. He stopped and then said to her, "It's ok. You're going to be fine." Tom quickly went to the door and looked through the peephole. His hunch had been right. No one was standing outside the door. He figured they wouldn't stand guard outside as it would draw attention. His bet was on them waiting in the lobby or outside in a vehicle.

Tom moved quickly and knelt in front of her. "What's your name?"

The girl shyly looked up at him and said, "Lin."

"Lin, I'm Tom. I'm not going to hurt you. I know what these men did to you and I'm going to get you back home."

Lin suddenly looked up at him wide-eyed and panicked. "No no no no. They will kill my parents!"

"Lin, I promise you nothing will happen to your parents, but you have to do exactly as I say, okay?"

"Are you a policeman?" she asked.

"No, not exactly. I'm a friend." Tom cupped her trembling hands and started to pull her up off the couch and she began to cry. "Lin, please come with me. We don't have much time. It's going to be okay."

Reluctantly, Lin rose from the couch with Tom's help and he ushered her out of the living room and into the bedroom. He walked over to the adjoining door and gave a cryptic knock. Lin looked on wearily as the locks on the doors were released and the door opened. Tom and Lin scooted into the adjoining suite.

"We have two hours."

Amy shook her head in acknowledgment and wrapped her arm over Lin and led her to the bed. "Ok. Let's get started."

Playing Videos

Hawthorne sat in the El Camino High School digital studio where students learned how to produce podcasts and tv broadcasting. One of the students was showing Hawthorne the video of Kent's speech in the gymnasium. He watched the video, but there was nothing to see. Kent had been standing at a podium and there were empty bleachers behind him. The camera was on a fixed tripod, so when Kent got off the podium the shot didn't follow him.

"Do you have any other footage of this guy from that night?"

"I have some B-roll that one of the students shot. It was never edited together, so it's just random shots."

"Let's have a look," said Hawthorne.

The student dragged another folder onto the computer desktop then clicked on it and opened a file. He dropped it into the timeline of Adobe Premiere and hit the play button. They both watched in silence. After about five minutes of random shots of the party-goers, Hawthorne asked the kid if he could speed up the video. The student, eager to impress him, showed him how he could go anywhere in the timeline.

He darted around looking for any shots of Kent and finally found one. He backed up and played it at normal speed.

"He's the guy who got killed, right?"

"You heard about that?"

"Yeah, everyone heard about it. It was the talk of the school. They said it was a gruesome kill. Did you see the body?"

"No, I didn't."

"Oh. I thought that's why you were here," said the disappointed student.

"I'm actually interested in who he was with that night." There was a quick shot of Kent and his group before it veered off in a different direction. "Wait, can you pause there."

"Sure thing."

The student scrubbed back to the shot and stopped. Hawthorne could make out Kent, two big guys, and a couple of girls huddled together.

"Can you zoom in?"

"You bet," said the kid, who was excited that the cop was excited. He was in a roundabout way helping out on a murder investigation. At least that's what he was going to tell his buddies.

"Is there a way to get a snapshot of that and print it out?"

"Sure, no problem." The kid took a screenshot and saved it and then sent it to the printer.

Hawthorne told the kid to let the video play some more and he sat back and watched. Just as he was getting ready to get up and leave something caught his eye on the computer screen. "Wait, stop!"

The kid stopped the video.

"Zoom in. What the hell?" Hawthorne leaned in toward the computer screen and squinted his eyes. One of the big guys that had been with Kent was now with a different group. In the group was an attractive blond in a blue dress and a tall, handsome man. Although he had only caught a quick glimpse of his face when he briefly removed his sunglasses, he was sure this was the same guy who had been on the plane. "Do you know who that guy is?" asked Hawthorne.

"I have no idea. But Mrs. Stratton, whom you met earlier, might know. She's been around here since before the dinosaurs."

"Print that for me."

"Is he the killer?" asked the kid.

Hawthorne stared at the screen, his hand rubbing his chin. He was wondering the same thing.

Escape

A well-dressed couple and their daughter exited the elevator into the lobby of the Fairmont Hotel. The woman had on a long white summer dress, long brunette hair, bright red lipstick, big round Dolce Gabbana sunglasses, and a large white summer hat. The man was also dressed in casual summer attire: khaki slacks, Tommy Hilfiger light blue shirt, and aviator sunglasses. The daughter had short blond hair, a white summer dress with big sunflowers on it, and big sunglasses to match her big hat. They turned in the lobby, and instead of heading to the front doors went down a hallway toward the pool. The trio passed a large Samoan man who was sitting on a couch, talking on a cell phone.

Just before the pool, they turned down a hallway off to their left. The hallway led to a couple of glass doors that led to the street. They exited and hurried down the street to a parking garage and entered and went past several rows of cars until they came to a grey SUV. Tom unlocked the vehicle and Amy and Lin got in.

"There's a police department a couple of miles from here. I've already programmed the location in the GPS. Go there and let them know who this is and let them take it from there. Then get back to LA. The ticket is in the glove box."

"You're not coming with us?"

"No, I have some unfinished business."

Amy stared at Tom and then gave him a hug and kiss. "Be careful."

"Always," replied Tom.

Amy started the SUV, checked the GPS, then looked over at Lin who was belted in. Amy backed the SUV out of the parking stall and drove toward the exit as Tom looked on.

Once the SUV had exited the parking structure, Tom unlocked the car door to the sedan that had been parked next to the SUV. He got in and turned on the GPS that would get him to Kent's house. It was time to hack into Kent's computer and see what he could find. The only problem was Gilman wasn't at the hotel. Where was he?

Waiting for Hitsman

Gilman banked the eight ball off the left side of the pool table but missed the pocket. He was randomly shooting pool on Kent's pool table thinking he might be able to make some room for it back at his place since Kent wouldn't be needing it anymore. His cell phone vibrated, and he scooped it out of his pocket.

"Was it him?"

"It looked like him, but I'm not sure. It's been a while since the reunion."

"Did you get a photo?"

"Yeah, Boss. I'll send it to you now." Moro looked up and saw a family walking past him down the hall. They were dressed like tourists with big hats and flowery skirts. He had nothing against tourists except when they went out of their way to look like idiot tourists. He pulled the photo up of Tom and sent it to Gilman.

Gilman received the photo and opened it up. It was him! What luck. "Is he still in the room?"

"Yeah, Boss. I told him two hours."

"Great, keep him there. I'm on my way."

Gilman tossed the pool cue down onto the table and picked up the beer from the bar and swallowed the last gulps. He was pleased that Tom was with one of his girls. Maybe he would become a regular customer. Maybe he had other friends he could bring to the party. Maybe he could even use it as blackmail and get a shot at his hot Aussie girlfriend. Heck, maybe they could be friends again like in high school. The possibilities were endless. He scooped up his coat as he walked out of the game room and headed down the hallway.

Gilman raced his Cadillac SUV down the winding roads and then roared onto Market Street and sped toward the hotel. In a cluster of cars coming up Market Street opposite to Gilman, a grey sedan slowed as it got to the exit that would take him up the streets that Gilman had just come down. Tom checked the navigation on his GPS. He was less than a mile away from Kent's place. He took the next exit and navigated up the winding roads. Tom slowed down as he got close to the house and drove past, scoping it out. No cars were parked in the driveway or curbside. He continued past the house and looked for a place to park. He found a spot near a large garbage container from some construction being done on a house. He angled his car in front of the container and parked, then pulled out his custom PC laptop from a backpack and fired it up. Finding Kent's house had been easy. He had also accessed the layout of the house and retrieved the specs and serial numbers for the security cameras that were inside and outside of his house. Hacking into the security cameras and disarming the security would be easy since they were hooked up to the internet. Tom scanned the wifi connections and found the one for the cameras. He then ran a program he had created, and the screen flickered a bunch of numbers and letters. He clicked the program open, and his screen showed four partitions with a different camera view in each frame. He checked each of the areas in the camera's view and determined no one was home. He closed the laptop and put it in the backpack before getting out of the car and swinging the backpack around his shoulder and heading to Kent's house.

Connecting the Dots

Natalie uploaded the photo that Hawthorne had sent her into the facial recognition program the NCIC had recently set up for law enforcement agencies to use. The National Crime Information Center database was created in 1967 under FBI director J. Edgar Hoover. The purpose of the system was to create a centralized information system to facilitate information flow between the numerous law enforcement branches. Now it was much easier for law enforcement to use because of the modern technology readily available.

Although the facial recognition database was still in its infancy, it had been drastically improved by the cooperation of a social media company that had given them access to their algorithms, leading to a decree of a public outcry over its privacy and use. However, it had helped solve a couple of crimes in its first two years of operation. Hawthorne had a hunch, and in police work hunches were always good.

It wasn't a perfect photo of the guy, but she did notice he had attractive features. Apparently, there might be some kind of connection between Clark and Kent. Natalie hit start and let the program run while she strolled to the break room and poured herself a cup of coffee. She sat in one of the chairs sipping her coffee and looking through some of the photos that Hawthorne had texted her. Then she had an idea. She went back to the detective room and sat at her desk, looking through the case file, skimmed her finger down one of the pages, and stopped. She picked up the phone and dialed.

"Hi, Mrs. Clark. How are you? It's Detective Martinez. I was wondering if I might be able to text you a photo to see if you recognize the person. Ok, great. I'll send it over now."

Natalie loaded the picture and then sent it to Helen Clark's cell phone. As she was doing this, the computer program came back with a hit on the photo. Natalie stared at the face and the information next to it.

"Hi, Detective. I don't recognize the face."

"Ok, thank you," said Natalie.

"Detective, is there any progress on my husband's case?"

"No, not yet. But we are working on some leads."

"What kind of—" Natalie hung up on Helen in mid-sentence as her attention had been drawn to the face on the computer screen. Next to the face was the name, Thomas J. Hitsman. She pulled out her cell phone and hit the speed dial.

****

It turned out that the old dinosaur's memory wasn't as sharp as it used to be in the Jurassic Era as she didn't recognize the handsome reunion guest from the photo. However, she did have Kent Lim's address on file since they had been corresponding with him for the recent reunion.

Hawthorne was now on his way to Kent's house when his cell phone chirped. "Hey, any luck with the photo?"

"Actually, yeah. We lucked out. Turns out your friend has done quite a bit of contract work for the government, so he was in the system."

"What kind of work?"

"From what I can tell he is some kind of cybersecurity expert."

"What does that mean?" asked Hawthorne.

"He's probably a white hat hacker."

"A what?" asked Hawthorne.

"It means he's good with computers. Really good," replied Natalie. "You said you met this guy on the plane and he was also at the reunion?"

"Yeah. Some coincidence, right?"

"I don't believe in coincidences," said Natalie. "Did he tell you what he was in town for?"

"Sounded like he has some medical issues. Possibly terminal."

"What if this guy is partnered with these guys? Or worse, what if he's the killer?"

The same thought had crossed his mind. "What's his name?" asked Hawthorne.

"Thomas Hitsman. I'll send you the info. I'll also start a background on him and let you know what I find."

Hawthorne recalled the guy had said his name was John. Hawthorne clenched his teeth. "Ok, let me know what you find."

Breaking and Exiting

Shards of glass splintered and bounced onto the tile floor like jagged little diamonds. Tom had just shattered the small laundry door window on the backside of the house. He looked around to make sure no neighbors had seen, then reached in through the broken hole in the window and unlocked the door. He slipped in quickly and closed the door behind him, put the tire iron back into his backpack, and hurried out of the laundry room area to the hallway which led to main rooms, including the office.

Tom found the office and scooted in quickly. He looked at the nice view then sat behind the desk and nudged the mouse on Kent's computer. The computer came to life. Someone had left it on. He moved the mouse, and a password window came up. He bent down to reach for his backpack to pull out a password descrambler when he noticed a sticky note on the floor. He picked it up and figured he might be in luck because it looked like a password. He typed the password in, and the computer unlocked and came to life. Tom checked his watch to see how much more time he had before they discovered he and the girl were missing.

Forty-five minutes. He stuck a thumb drive into Kent's computer and started searching to see what he could find.

****

Amy was reluctant to give any more information to the San Francisco cops other than the girl was one who had been reported missing in Southern California. While the cops were talking with the girl verifying her story, Amy slipped out of the police station and quickly walked back to the lot where she had parked the SUV. She got in and reached behind the seat and pulled out her purse. She rummaged in her purse and then frantically began opening all the inner and side pockets of the purse. She was looking for her cell phone. "Shit!" Suddenly she remembered. The last time she saw it was on the side table in the hotel room. She reached in the purse and pulled out the airline ticket Tom had bought her. The flight didn't depart for another three hours. If she hurried, she could return to the hotel and get her cell phone and still make the flight back to Los Angeles. She was only a few miles from the hotel.

****

Tom did a search for jpegs and hit the jackpot. He opened a file folder called *Talent* and started going through the photographs. The photos were of various young girls. Most were Asian, but there were other ethnicities. There were headshots and sexy poses. He scrolled down the list of hundreds of photos, copying each to his flash drive. He continued poking through the various files and found an Excel sheet with names and photos and an address next to each photo.

He Googled the addresses and found that many of them were nail salons. He thought about it and concluded that the girls were working day jobs at the various nail salons and then working as sex slaves on their off time and weekends. He copied the Excel sheet over to the flash drive. A sharp buzz startled him. He looked around and noticed the security monitor on the edge of the desk. The monitor was for the security camera aimed at the front door entrance. Tom scooted his chair closer and took a look at the man who had just rung the doorbell. The man looked like Hawthorne, the detective from the plane. *What the heck was he doing here?*

Hawthorne buzzed the door again. Tom could see him looking around. He tried the door to see if it was open, then looked up at the camera. For a moment, Tom had the sensation that Hawthorne could see him staring back at him. Hawthorne turned and then walked back up the pathway. Tom realized he had been holding his breath. He exhaled and then moved the chair back and pulled the flash drive from the computer. He maneuvered himself over to the room next to the office where he could catch a glimpse from one of the small windows out the side of the house. He had a feeling Hawthorne would do exactly what he had done, work his way to the back. This guy was tenacious. Sure enough, within a minute he caught Hawthorne walking past the side of the house.

Tom thought fast. If Hawthorne saw the broken window, chances are he would come inside, so he headed for the front door, hurrying out of the house. No alarm sounded. He swiftly jogged up the front pathway and then turned right and ran up the street to where he had parked his car. He got to his car, opened the door, and threw his backpack into the passenger seat before jumping into the driver's seat. Time to roll.

****

Gilman walked into the lobby and found Moro sitting on a sofa playing games on his iPhone. Biehn was sitting next to him.

"How long has it been?"

"Hey, Boss. Yeah, it's been about two hours."

"Let's go up and say hello," said Gilman.

Moro motioned to Biehn to stay behind. Gilman and Moro arrived at the floor and exited the elevator and walked down the hallway to the end where the suite was located. Moro knocked. They waited over a minute and then Moro knocked again. They looked at each other.

"Call him," said Gilman.

Moro called and waited, there was no answer. Gilman was antsy as he couldn't wait to welcome Tom to the club. After allowing five minutes to go by, Gilman nodded to Moro. Moro pulled out a key card and pressed it to the door lock and the lock disengaged. Moro had made it a practice that whenever they delivered girls to the hotels, they would bribe one of the bellboys for a key to the room. They would only use it if something went wrong or if one of the girls that wasn't allowed to be bruised was being mistreated. They had different girls for different clients. Some were strictly for sexual gratification, some were for the sadist clientele that enjoyed bondage and beating the girls. If the clients ever beat one of the wrong girls, they usually got a beating from Moro.

Moro pushed the door open, and they went in. Gilman had a big grin, which soon diminished. The living room area was empty. They looked around, and Gilman peeled off to the bedroom. It was empty as well. Moro followed in after checking the rest of the suite.

"Where are they?" asked Gilman.

"I don't know. They never came down to the lobby."

They both stood silent in wonderment. The bed was still made, nothing was out of order. Suddenly they heard a ring tone chime. Gilman looked around and moved in the general direction of the incoming chime. He noticed that the door that connected the bedroom suite to an adjoining room was ajar. He moved closer to it and the chime grew louder. He pushed the door open a bit more and saw a cell phone chiming on a dresser. Then it stopped. Just then a woman in a summer dress and big hat walked into the bedroom and over to the dresser and picked up the phone. She turned as she was looking down at the missed call. Gilman recognized her immediately and his face lit up.

"Miss Australia, we meet again."

Amy's heart skipped a beat as she looked up and saw a grinning Gilman standing in the doorway to the adjacent room. She froze for a beat then bolted. Gilman shoved the door wide open, and he and Moro barreled through, giving chase to the frightened gazelle.

She ran into the living room suite and out the main door and made a hard right into the hallway and ran as fast as her high heels would allow her as Gilman spurted out of the door close behind. She made it to the end of the hallway and turned down the next hallway and almost ran into a cart full of toiletries and towels. She swung the cart into the middle and kept running. Gilman took the turn like a bull running down the village streets of Spain and crashed directly into the cart, sending the contents flying. Like a true linebacker, he tried to steamroll through, but his foot got tangled and he took a header onto the floor. Moro took the turn and managed to dodge the mess. Gilman pulled out his cell phone and hit the speed dial as Moro continued down the hallway.

Amy ran up to the elevator bank and pushed the buttons with the freight train Moro hot on her tail. She eyed the stairwell and sprinted in that direction just as Moro caught up and clipped her on the ankle, causing her to lose her balance and tumble to the floor. Moro, who was packing some extra weight, overestimated his agility and speed, lost his footing, and also tumbled to the floor right behind Amy. Amy started to get up, but Moro grabbed her ankle. She saw he was on the ground behind her and as he pulled her towards him she kicked back with her free foot, gouging him in the eye with her high heel. Moro yelped and let go of her as he covered his face.

Amy frantically got up on her feet and ran into the stairway. She scrambled down each step as fast as she could until she came to the main floor door. She exited the door and stopped momentarily to get her bearings, and suddenly she felt an electrical charge surge through her body. Everything went black.

Biehn slipped the Taser back into his pocket and looked around, making sure no one had just witnessed him sticking the two-pronged Taser into the side of Amy's neck. He knelt to pick her up as Moro came through the door. Moro gave Biehn a head nod then scooped up Amy and carried her limp body away.

****

Hawthorne worked his way to the back of the house. The gravel was loose, as the house was built on an incline, which caused him to slip, but he regained his balance. He hoisted himself up onto a deck and then saw a broken window on a door. He looked in and saw that it was the laundry room. He had his hand on the doorknob when his phone rang. He quickly reached in his pocket to silence the phone. He pulled it out and answered when he saw it was Natalie.

"I'm a bit busy," Hawthorne answered in a low, hushed tone.

"I hope you are not going off-book. I just found something that I think may link Hitsman to Lim. If I'm right, it may link back to Clark."

"What is it?"

"It has to do with one of the shell companies that rented the warehouse. But I'm waiting on confirmation. I just wanted to give you a heads-up so you don't do something to compromise the case."

"Ok, thanks. I'll call you later." Hawthorne put the phone back in his pocket and stared at the shattered glass. He wouldn't be going in. No, it would be a better idea to get back to the hotel and find out what John…or Tom was really up to—right now, he was prime suspect number one.

****

Tom plugged in an address into the GPS and continued following the directions. Twenty minutes later, he was at a mini-mall off of Market Street. He looked around at the several small businesses, many of which were electronic stores, but in the corner was MiMi's Nail Salon. He pulled into an empty stall and then walked over to the salon. He looked through the glass doors and saw several women working on various clients' hands and feet. He pulled the door open and walked in and up to the front counter. He tried to get a look at the women, but most had their back to him as they worked on the clients. Finally, one got up and came over and greeted him. She was an older Asian woman who spoke in broken English.

"You want nails, massage, or pedicure?"

Tom looked up at the chalkboard menu and saw that neck and shoulder massages were also on the list. "Massage."

"Follow," said the decrepit old lady as she led him to a chair in the corner.

Tom settled into the chair, and the old bird made him rest his face on the rubber face placemat that was attached to the massage chair. As a girl walked over to work on him, he pulled his face up from the mat, looked around, and asked her if he could use the bathroom. She motioned to the back of the shop and said it was to the right.

Tom went to the back and through the door, but instead of going to the right he took a left and went down a hallway. When he got to the end, he opened a door and took a quick look. It led to a stairway to the second floor of the salon. He went up the stairs and then started down the hallway. When he came to the first door, he tried the knob. It was unlocked, so he pushed it open. There was a single bed and small side dresser and a table and lamp in the corner. He closed it and moved to the next door and peeked inside, where he saw the same thing. As he closed the door another one further down the hallway opened and a young Asian girl stepped out into the hallway. She was startled when she saw him, but then slowly walked up to him. She was wearing a tank top and red workout shorts.

"You look for girl?" she asked him in her broken English.

"No, I, uh, I was looking for the bathroom."

She smiled at him. "Bathroom downstairs." She pointed back toward the stairs.

He nodded and thanked her.

On his way back to the hotel, Tom called Amy but got her voicemail. He figured she was probably boarding the plane. His plan was to go back to the hotel and figure out his next move. He had information that he could and would turn over to the authorities at the right time, but first, he had to go over his plan for Gilman. Of course, Gilman would now be alerted, but he may not know the entire details. Then he remembered the photo. The giant Samoan had taken a photo of him and had probably shown it to Gilman by now, so the advantage of surprise was off the table.

Half an hour later, Tom was staring at his phone back in his hotel room. Three calls had not been answered by Amy. She should have checked in by now. His phone chirped, and it was a Facetime request from Amy. *About time*, he thought. He answered and was startled when he saw the horrific image on his phone. It was Gilman's big grinning face.

"Hi, Tommy. You left so soon I didn't get a chance to catch up with you. And you took property that belongs to me. That wasn't very nice."

"Cut the bullshit, Darren. Where's Amy?"

Gilman chuckled, bemused at how authoritative Tom was trying to sound. "You know, Tommy, you really aren't as fun as you used to be in high school. You're so serious now. Ok, then…." Gilman shifted the view on the phone to show Amy tied up in a chair. She had a gag in her mouth and looked pissed off as opposed to terrified, which gave Tom a bit of a reprieve from the knot he was feeling in his stomach. "She has a bit of a mouth on her, so I had to quiet her down. Too bad, cause I like that Aussie accent of hers."

"What do you want?"

"What do I want? I want my girl back, Tommy. She's special. Just like Amy."

Apparently, Gilman didn't know that the girl had been turned over to the police, and Amy had not given that up so Tom still might have the strategic advantage.

"I'm listening."

"Kent has a house here in town. I'll text you the address. Six o'clock. Bring the girl."

The phone cut off.

Blowfish Moro

Dusk shadows stretched out across the streets of the Twin Peaks neighborhood as Tom parked near Kent's house. He walked into Kent's house after being buzzed in and felt like a cow heading to slaughter. Just a few hours earlier he had been there. If that damn detective had not shown up, he could have stayed there and surprised Gilman. Maybe he would have hit him in the toothy grin with the tire iron and knocked out his teeth. Although he still would have had to deal with that big Samoan. He went inside and was greeted by a young Vietnamese man with a limp who led him down the hallway to the game room where Moro was waiting for him. Moro was dressed in black like one of Elvis' Memphis mafia guys, wearing black sunglasses and his hair slicked back into a ponytail.

"Where's the girl?" asked Moro.

"She's safe. Where's Amy?" responded Tom.

Moro grinned. "She's safe."

Suddenly, the door behind Tom closed and he heard a lock turn. He quickly glanced back and then focused back on Moro. "So, this is the way it's going to be?"

"Yeah, bro." Moro took a step toward him.

Tom took a step back. "You're not going to get your girl back if you kill me."

"We have more," said Moro, taking another step toward him.

"Yes, and I know where they are being kept. I have all the addresses of your safe houses and nail salons."

Moro didn't flinch. "We're moving them."

Tom stepped back and bumped into the side of the pool table. He reached back and felt a pool cue, and just as Moro lunged forward he swung the pool cue and slammed it into the side of Moro's head. The pool cue snapped in half, leaving a jagged end in Tom's fist, but before he could react Moro punched him in the gut and swiftly picked him up like a rag doll and tossed him up and over the pool table. Tom landed with a thud and felt sharp pain spread like a spider web across his right hip. Gasping for breath and reeling from the pain, he slowly dragged himself about a foot on the tile floor until he felt a big pair of hands grab him by the scruff of his neck and around his belt, and he was airborne again. He crashed into the wall, and several photos that were hanging crashed down on top of him.

Tom reached up to a cabinet next to him and pulled himself up and turned just in time to catch one of Moro's elbows directly to the face, which sent him flying onto the floor. Tom knew instinctively that he could defend himself with a thumb to the eye or a kick to the knee, but that initial blow to his gut had left him breathless and on the defensive. Moro picked up the cabinet and launched it at Tom. *Jesus, this guy isn't giving me a chance.*

The cabinet missed him and crashed into the fish tank, shattering it and sending hundreds of gallons of water cascading onto the floor. The cabinet exploded and scuba gear spilled everywhere. Tom scrambled on his knees over the wet floor and gear, away from Moro. His adrenalin had kicked in and he wasn't feeling the pain anymore, and wasn't sure if he was breathing, but he was still alive.

One of the triggerfish was flopping around, and Tom managed to grab it and fling it at Moro. Moro caught the fish in midair like a bear catching a salmon. He grinned and took a bite out of the fish and swallowed it, tossing the limp, dead fish aside. Tom grimaced and turned, scurrying across the soaked floor and gear. He came to a wall and turned sideways and slid up onto his feet as Moro reached out to grab his face with his right giant hand. Simultaneously, Tom slammed his right fist into the side of Moro's face. Moro stopped in his tracks with a frozen grin at Tom's feeble attempt to punch him in the face. It took him about two seconds to realize that Tom had jammed the WASP military knife into his jaw and up into the roof of his mouth. Before he could counter strike Tom's arm, Tom pushed the button on the knife. A burst of sub-zero CO2 gas exploded at 800 psi into Moro's giant head, giving him the worst case of brain freeze he had ever experienced. Moro's body went into shock and Tom yanked out the knife and was about to stab him in the jugular, but as if in slow motion, Moro toppled over and fell with a horrendous thud onto the floor. Moro's eyes were still open, and he still had that stupid grin on his frozen face.

Tom sighed, stepped back, and tossed the knife aside. Moro's shoulder holster was exposed, and Tom reached down and pulled out the Glock-17 and checked it. He had one at home, but it had been a couple of months since he had gone to the range. He was familiar enough with it to use it if backed into a corner. And now he had to use it. He fired a shot at Moro's head just for good measure. He didn't want this monster getting up again like always happened in the horror movies. Fuck him.

There was only one way out, and that door had been locked, so Tom took aim and blew out the lock. He carefully pulled the door open and took a quick peek, and was greeted with two bullets whizzing past his head and slamming into the door frame above him, splintering wood. He quickly ducked back. He heard footsteps running toward the front of the house. Whoever had just shot at him was escaping. He bolted into the hallway with the Glock at the ready. Clear both ways. He hugged the wall as he quickly made his way down the hallway toward the front of the house. He got to the living room and took a quick peek. The front door was left ajar. He scrambled outside and up the walkway just in time to see a white van skidding out down the street. Tom ran up the street and jumped into his rental. He revved it up and took off after the van. It was dark now, but he could see the taillights of the van about two blocks ahead of him racing through the neighborhood.

Biehn was making a right turn and suddenly hit the brakes and skidded to a stop, creasing a parked car. A mini tour bus was coming up the street he needed to turn onto to get out of the neighborhood and head downtown. The tour bus stopped abruptly. There was no way to get around it on these narrow streets, so Biehn cursed and slammed the van into reverse and then continued up the street as Tom gained on him. Biehn and Tom continued up the curvy streets to the top of the scenic Twin Peaks. Biehn was driving recklessly and almost hit some people who were exiting their car.

At 922 feet in elevation, Twin Peaks is second only to Mt. Davidson in height in the San Francisco area, offers spectacular views of the Bay Area, and is a world-famous tourist attraction. Originally called "Los Pechos de la Choca" (Breasts of the Maiden) by early Spanish settlers, these two adjacent peaks provide postcard views and a treasure trove of animal and plant diversity.

Biehn couldn't give a shit about postcard views or the tourists jumping out of his way as he careened his van around the curves and raced to the top. He had spotted Tom giving chase and wasn't about to get caught by this imbecile who had managed to kill Moro. He had been sitting in the living room on Kent's big white couch and had heard the destruction coming from the game room. He would have liked to have seen Moro ripping Tom apart limb by limb, but had agreed he would wait outside in case anyone came to the front, and also to prepare the tarp to wrap up Tom's body. He was very surprised when he heard the shot and instead of Moro coming out he saw that bastard stick his head out. At least he got a couple of shots off even if they missed. He had never shot at a human before, but had always had an inkling do so. He just wished he had a chance to take better aim.

Biehn rounded the last curve and came to a screeching halt and collided with another car. The parking area was full of tourists enjoying the windy but clear and scenic night. Biehn was confused and wasn't sure which way to go. There were cars and buses everywhere. Some angry people approached him for crashing into the car, and Biehn jumped out of the van and stuck his gun in their faces. "Fuck off!" he shouted, and the people quickly backed away. Tom rounded the corner and hit his brakes, skidding to a stop. Biehn turned and fired a shot at his car and hit the windshield. People screamed and started to scatter. Biehn turned and hobbled through the throng of cars toward one of the peaks.

Tom was caught by surprise when the bullet impacted the windshield. Damn, that was the second time this guy had almost blown his head off. This maniac was really starting to piss him off. He didn't want to kill him because he needed to find out where they were holding Amy, but he didn't want to get killed either. He saw Biehn scurrying through the throng of cars and people but lost track of him as he bailed out of his rental. Tom crouched as he ran from one car to the next, keeping his head low while trying to spot the Vietnamese menace. He heard some screams ahead and to the right, most likely from a tourist who had encountered the menace.

He looked off to his left and could see the sparkling lights of the city below and the silhouettes of people running past him. He continued in the direction from which the people were running. He peered out from behind the bumper of a bus and caught the dark shape limping off onto a trail. He quickly scooted next to a row of cars, keeping low to the ground, popping up in time to see Biehn heading toward the lip of the peak.

Biehn limped up the trail of wooden dilapidated steps toward the top, knocking a couple of teen girls to the side as he bullied his way past them. One of them yelled at him and he turned and fired a shot at her, which narrowly missed her head. They screamed and scrambled down the hillside. Biehn continued up.

Tom broke into a run across the parking lot toward the stairs as the girls reached the bottom. "Are you ok?"

"He shot at me!" yelled the terrified teen as she and her friend ran past him.

Tom started up the rickety steps, trying to take two at a time. As he reached the top, he felt a hot whiz fly past his ear and then heard the crack of a pistol a fraction of a second later. He dove to his right and rolled and settled in the dirt. He strained his neck as he peered up to see if he could spot Biehn. He saw a flicker of light bounce off a stripe on the jacket that Biehn was wearing. Tom could see he was behind the leg of a giant antenna that was on the peak. Tom took aim and fired a shot. Sparks exploded as the bullet ricochet off the steel frame of the antenna.

Biehn flinched and took off running across the dark ground. He was getting close to the other side where he could run down the hill and get to the road and possibly hijack a car, when suddenly his foot sunk into the ground and got jammed. In an instant, he was engulfed in a buzzing cloud of angry hornets. Biehn had stepped right into their nest, and boy were they pissed. He wrenched his ankle as he tried to get away but fell to the ground as his foot was still stuck in the hole. The stinging was intense. Like fireballs boring into his skin as they attacked him and stung him all over his body. He yelled, and two flew into his mouth and stung his tongue. His right eye was swollen shut. In sheer desperation, Biehn ripped his foot free and frantically stumbled away from the hive, but the hornets swarmed him. He was in excruciating pain and could barely see as he came to the edge of the peak and tumbled over and careened down the hill, flipping head over feet. When he came to rest at the bottom most of the hornets had dissipated. Unable to see, he crawled forward on his hands and knees as the few remaining hornets fell free. Biehn suddenly felt the cool asphalt under his hands. A hornet stung his neck and he feebly brushed it off. His hands scratched at the ground as he half crawled and half pulled himself further onto the asphalt. He placed his face onto the asphalt, his cheek pressing down into the road. It felt so cool compared to the raging heat the rest of his body was experiencing. Through the slit of his one good eye, he saw a flash of light rush toward him as the police cruiser rounded the corner. He didn't feel any more heat or coolness as the tire of the police SUV ran over his head, splattering it like a watermelon.

Tom had seen Biehn waving his hands like a madman and then hobbling frantically away from a shadowy cloud. At first, he didn't understand what was going on, but then he had heard the rumbling buzz from the mad hornets and realized Biehn was under attack. He angled off to his left to avoid getting stung. He thought he might be able to flank him if he found another way down, and then he saw the red and blue lights flickering in the distance coming up the snaking road. It was time to get out of there. The cars were now starting to pile up behind one another as everyone was trying to leave and the police were trying to arrive. It was turning into a cluster fuck, which was good, because he could slip away in the confusion.

By the time Tom made it back to his car it was one of the few left in the parking area. There was a bullet hole in the windshield, which wasn't good, so he decided to abandon it.

He had used his fake ID to rent it, so he didn't care. He ended up hitching a ride with a young couple from Denmark. As they slowly followed the cars down the road the way he had driven up he wondered if the maniac had gotten away. The couple drove him back to his hotel and they were very ecstatic after he set them up with a room. They also understood that it was probably best they didn't recall giving him a lift should anyone ask.

The Shootout

A slice of morning sun slipped through the plantation blinds and played on Tom's face, stirring him awake. After a restless night of pacing back and forth he finally drifted off to sleep from exhaustion. His head was in a groggy mist as he rubbed his eyes when suddenly his synapses kicked in and the events of the previous night tumbled into his consciousness. He snapped up in bed. He still had his clothes and shoes on as he threw his legs over the side of the bed and stumbled to the bathroom. When he walked into the living room area, he took a peek out the window. He expected to see the cops swarming on the street below and scrambling up to his room, but he knew he was most likely in the clear. He took a quick shower and then ordered some room service. He went through his duffle bag checking the special items he had brought for his buddy Gilman. He knew he would find a way to use them, but first he had to save Amy.

****

Natalie walked down the terminal at SFO toward the arrival gate. She was tired from the flight where she only managed to sleep sporadically in between watching reruns of *Friends*, one of her favorite shows. Her current Netflix binge was *Bosch*, about an LAPD detective who battled bad guys on the streets while battling the inner workings of the Los Angeles Police Department at the same time. It was one of those shows that, although fantasy, was also grounded in realism and truth. She was proud that she was a detective serving her community and catching bad guys just like the make-believe Bosch.

She got her rental car and put the address to Hawthorne's hotel into her cell phone and followed the instructions. She had not told Hawthorne she was flying out with some new leads. Part of it was that she wanted to get some of the credit for the case and get into the action, and part of it was that she wanted to see San Francisco. It was about a twenty-four-mile drive from SFO, which was actually situated in the city of Burlingame, an upper middle-class suburban neighborhood. Natalie realized she was hungry but decided to wait until she got to the hotel. She was excited about the information she had for Hawthorne.

Tom was finishing up his breakfast when his phone chimed with a text. He checked and saw it was from Gilman: *I underestimated you, Tommy. If you want to see Amy alive, meet me tonight at the gym. 8 sharp.*

Tom delighted knowing he would finally get to go one on one with that thug Gilman. Getting Amy back would also be a good thing, but not as thrilling as getting revenge on

Gilman. But first he had to make a couple of calls and disrupt some businesses. Deep down he knew he had changed, or as he reasoned, he had adapted to his new situation. Never in a million years would he have thought he would one day be committing homicide. Multiple homicides. *And well planned,* he thought to himself. But as he had reasoned months before, why should he die and these scumbags continue living? They were bad guys. Sex traffickers. The world wouldn't miss them. He wondered if he would have done the same thing if he didn't have terminal cancer. It was too late to ponder. He was committed and had to see it through. Gilman had to die.

Hawthorne walked up to the front desk in the lobby of the Fairmont and flashed his badge to the young lady typing into her computer and showed her a photo and asked if the man was registered there. He gave her the name Thomas Hitsman. She typed in her computer and said there was no one registered under that name. He was about to try a possible alias Natalie had discovered when he looked in the mirror behind the front desk and saw Tom exit the elevator and cross the lobby toward the parking lot. He watched him in the mirror.

"Is there anything else?" asked the woman behind the counter.

"No, thanks."

Hathorne walked toward the front of the hotel and glanced at Tom far down the hallway exiting toward the parking lot. Hawthorne picked up the pace and jogged out the front of the hotel and down the street. He had parked on the street half a block from the exit to the parking garage. He got to his rental car, and just as he got in, he saw Tom exit the parking garage in an SUV. Hawthorne started the car and veered away from the curb, keeping some distance between himself and Tom.

Twenty minutes later, he had followed Tom into a small strip mall off Market Street. He parked a few rows over from where Tom parked and watched him get out of his car and walk into a nail salon. Hawthorne sat in his car and watched the front entrance. It was kind of early for a rub and tug, but to each his own. I suppose if you are terminal all bets are off as to how you behave and what you do with your time. Hawthorne pulled a stick of gum out of his coat pocket and stuck it in his mouth. He lowered the window and tossed out the wrapper.

Suddenly, Hathorne heard the familiar sound of cracking gunshots coming from what he thought was inside the massage parlor. He opened the door and quickly slid out of the car. He paused and listened, and he heard two more shots, and then the front door burst open and people ran out of the shop. He ran toward the door, dodging little Asian ladies, and pulled his weapon. He paused at the entrance and took a quick look into the establishment and then rushed in. Two muffled shots rang out from upstairs in the back. He ran toward the back and stopped at the door. He quickly pushed the door open and poked his head in and scanned the hallway. He saw a couple of bodies lying prone down the hallway. He spotted the stairs and started up them, taking them two steps at a time. A young Asian girl appeared at the top of the stairs, and he almost pulled the trigger. She shrieked, but then ran down the steps past him.

Hathorne stepped out onto the landing on the second floor and looked to his right. He saw doorways. He started down the hallway, and in a flash a person flew out of an open door and tackled him and knocked him into the open room directly across. At the exact same time a burst of gunfire opened up on them and barely missed them. As Hawthorne hit the floor, he realized he just narrowly escaped being ripped to shreds. Tom quickly rolled off of him and got to his feet and leaned up against the wall.

"He's got a mac ten. He's down in the last room on the right."

"How many more?" asked Hawthorne.

"Just one from what I can tell. Nice of you to join me."

"I had a couple of questions for you. My first one is...what did you get me into here?"

"Long story. The quick version is these are sex traffickers."

In the distance they heard the sirens getting closer.

"Given that we are outgunned, we stay put until the cavalry arrives unless he comes down the hallway toward us," said Hawthorne.

As he finished, there was a sound from down the hallway of what sounded like a door being opened and then slamming shut. Hawthorne looked at Tom.

"There's a backdoor emergency exit that leads to the alley. I checked it out yesterday," said Tom.

"You have a lot of explaining to do," said Hawthorne.

"It will have to wait," replied Tom.

"Stay here." Hawthorne took a quick look out the door. He then started down the hallway, then quickened his pace down until he reached the end and started down the stairway.

The sirens outside intensified. Hawthorne pushed open the door and stepped into the alley. He didn't see anyone.

Hawthorne went to go back in but couldn't open the emergency door. He had to walk all the way around the back of the strip mall to get back to the front. By the time he reached the front again, the cops were everywhere. He held out his badge as he approached the officer who was holding the perimeter. The officer let him through, and he walked up to the officer in command as some officers were coming out of the nail salon and the "all clear" was now being transmitted on the radios.

He showed his badge. "Did you get the shooter?"

The cop looked at his badge and said, "Just bodies." He eyed the detective again. "A little out of your jurisdiction."

The SFPD inspector that Hawthorne had met with a couple of days earlier pulled up in his sedan. He got out and walked over to both of them. "What do you have?" he asked the ranking cop.

"It's code-four now, but we have a bunch of shot-up dudes inside. Not sure who is who yet but it looks like it may have been a turf war or drug rip-off." The inspector turned his attention to Hawthorne. "What are you doing here?"

"Seems to be the question of the day," answered Hawthorne. He knew if he told the inspector he was involved he would get bogged down in the investigation, and he wanted to get back on the trail. "Just a coincidence. I just stopped to see if they need any help."

The inspector looked him over then turned to the cop on scene. "Was he inside?"

"No, Sir. He came from the other end of the parking lot."

"Looks like you got it under control." Hawthorne turned and started walking away.

The inspector eyed Hawthorne. "How's your investigation going?"

Hawthorne turned back. "Dead end. I'm going to play tourist for a day then head back to the cold."

The Inspector watched Hawthorne walk back down the parking lot toward his car.

Close to the End

Tom drove down Market Street until he got to O'Farrell Street, then turned left. He managed to get out of the building before the first patrol car rolled up on the scene and went undetected. He wasn't planning on getting into a shootout, but he was definitely glad he was armed and that the shooters were shitty shots. Unfortunately, he had not been able to scoop up any of the girls, and he hoped they did not end up back in the same situation. He had a different idea for the next stop. He found a parking spot in a small plaza. He saw the nail salon tucked away in the corner and spotted a pay phone at the other end of the l-shaped mall and decided that would be even better than using his disposable phone. He walked over and picked up the receiver and dialed 911.

"911, what is your emergency."

"Two men just walked into the Lin Nail Salon with guns. They are taking girls by force."

"Sir, what's your location?"

"It's at the Imperial Plaza on O'Farrell. Please hurry!"

"Sir what is your..."

Tom hung up, cutting her off, and walked back to his car and pulled out of the plaza. He could hear sirens in the distance. He figured with the shooting that just happened they would roll as fast as possible thinking this could be another mass shooting. It would cause a problem and disrupt Gilman's business. Tom smirked as he was heading back down toward Market Street and saw the incoming phalanx of police cars racing to the bogus shots fired scene. *Fuck Gilman*, he thought to himself. Tonight, all would be made right.

****

Gilman threw another vicious punch into the belly of the man tied to the chair. The man doubled over in pain, blood spilling from his mouth to the floor. Gilman followed up with a thunderous uppercut and nearly snapped the man's head off, the man's head bobbling from side to side like a broken top.

"Ehhh. You like that one, Miss Australia?"

Amy looked in horror at the broken man in the chair and back at Gilman's toothy grin. He had been beating him for five minutes, but it seemed like an eternity to Amy. She was sitting on the bed with her wrist handcuffed to the bedpost.

"If I wasn't so smitten with you, that might be you in that chair."

"You're sick," responded Amy.

"Ahhh. You don't think he deserves this? He lost an entire operation today, including two of my men. I'll tell you what, Australia, I'll let you pick where I center-punch him next."

Amy's face revolted. "What?"

"You tell me what part of his body I whack next. So, what's it going to be?"

"I'm not playing this game with you!" screamed Amy.

"If you don't play, then I'll have to end this and it will be your fault." Gilman walked over to the table and picked up the Mac-10 and aimed at the man's temple. "Three seconds, Australia."

The helpless bloody man locked eyes with Amy.

Amy groaned. "Ok, ok, stop." Her face was flush with anger and rage. "His knee," she quipped.

Gilman smiled. "His knee. I like that very much, Miss Australia."

Both Amy and the man sighed simultaneously. Gilman pulled the Mac-10 away from the man's temple then shot him in the knee. The man howled in pain, making more noise than the suppressor on the Mac-10.

"You son of a bitch! You said you were going to punch him!"

Gilman laughed heartily. "I did?" He quickly pointed the weapon at the man's head and fired a shot, exploding his brains on the wall behind him. Amy screamed but no sound came from her throat. Gilman walked toward her with the submachine gun at his side. "Don't feel so bad. He was never going to walk out of here. He fucked up. You can't be soft with your employees or they lose respect. Know what I mean?" Gilman put his hand under Amy's chin, and she pulled away. "Be nice now. Tommy won't be too happy if your face looks like a swollen melon when he sees you tonight."

A glimmer of hope sparked in Amy's eyes, but she didn't show Gilman her face.

****

Hawthorne returned to his hotel, and as he was walking through the lobby looking down at his cell phone, heard a familiar voice.

"You know you're gonna go blind if you keep looking at that tiny screen."

Hawthorne looked up and saw Natalie sitting in one of the comfortable oversized sofas in the lobby. "What are you doing here?"

"That's the welcome I get after I flew all night to save your ass?"

"I didn't know my ass needed saving. But you can tell me all about it over coffee. I've already had a hell of a day."

The Silver Beast

Gilman strapped Amy into the back seat of Kent's Humvee. Her hands and feet were bound, and she was on her side and seat-belted in so that she was not visible to anyone outside the Humvee. Gilman liked Kent's Humvee. It had a few extras, such as bulletproof armor plating and bulletproof windshield and windows. The coolest feature was a license plate that could be changed at the flip of a switch to a different identifier. It was something Kent had seen in a James Bond movie, and had paid some big bucks to have that mechanism installed. It was quite ingenious, and Gilman also had his Cadillac modified in the same way. Gilman felt invincible driving Kent's Humvee, and was elated that Kent wasn't around to protest. He was driving toward San Mateo, to the high school, planning on taking Tom on man to man. Just like back in high school. He figured it wasn't going to be too much of a challenge and he could just get the girl back and keep Amy for himself after he terminated Tom.

As Gilman came to the intersection of Junipero Serra and Sloat, he saw cars slowing down and commotion in the middle of the intersection. The intersection was quite big with a minimum of five different roads all merging together spread out over the length of half a football field. A couple of arteries led down toward the beach, while others led into the prestigious St. Francis Woods, and the road ahead continued to the freeway. As a few cars ahead of him entered the intersection he saw what the commotion was about. A group of protestors were marching through the intersection toward Grove Park. These were not your typical millennials jacked up on soy-milk lattes. These were fully funded and armed militia wearing the familiar black uniforms that had been terrorizing citizens for over a year. The white Mercedes in front of him was surrounded by a half a dozen as they gestured toward the driver to get out.

This pissed off Gilman. He scanned the area and saw no law enforcement. These domestic terrorists had been given a free pass by many and had grown emboldened. Even the local cops were afraid to go up against them for fear of retribution from the brass at their department. The police chiefs didn't want to lose their pensions and the mayors had their marching orders, thus the brunt of the political power play fell on the rank and file of the usually understaffed and underpaid police officers. So, they had to stand down when it came to the protestors. These groups were bad for business as well—especially his businesses. Things in society were slowly declining into the Wild West. He had not paid much attention to these anarchy imbeciles before because they had not directly affected him, but this was different. This was directly affecting him and was going to make him late to his destination.

One of the hooded militia aimed an AR-15 at the driver's window of the Mercedes while the others beat on the hood and kicked the side of the door panels. *Enough is enough*, Gilman thought to himself. These assholes had burned down one too many cities in his estimation, and now they were going to screw up his chance to kill Tom Hitsman.

Gilman reached to the dash that was adorned with lots of switches and panels. He pushed a button. The California license plate on the back of the Humvee switched, and a new one adorning Colorado plates took its place. He then leaned on the horn for a good five seconds.

The dozen or so protestors looked over at him. The man that was aiming the AR-15 at the Mercedes tilted his head like a dog as he looked at the silver Humvee. The Humvee then revved its engine in an angry display of irreverence at the group. The leader of the group nodded his head at the rest of them and they started toward the Humvee, falling into a haphazard line. Gilman continued to rev the Humvee's engine. The Humvee had tinted windows, so they couldn't see who the driver was as it slowly began creeping toward them. They stood in its path. The leader worked his way to the driver's door.

"Get out now." He motioned with his rifle like a third-world terrorist, waving at Gilman to exit the vehicle. Gilman revved the engine again. The group in front held the line. "I said get the fuck out now!" yelled the thug. The driver's side tinted window started to roll down and stopped at six inches. A fist emerged and pumped a fist. The leader took notice. "Roll down the window, brother."

The hand then rotated and quickly changed from a pumping fist to giving him the universal middle finger "fuck you" sign. The leader quickly raised his rifle to his shoulder, but the window quickly slid up. The Humvee then jerked forward with a roar and smashed into the four-militia standing in front. They were quickly shuddered and smashed as the Humvee ran over their bodies. The ones left standing opened fire on the Humvee and the sparks flew off the side panels and bounced off the tinted windows. The Humvee now in four-wheel drive, locked up the brake and spun in a fish tail, knocking down two more thugs, making them eat cement. Gilman then quickly reversed and ran over the bodies as they tried to get up off the ground. The angry tires bit into the pavement and raced forward, successfully mowing down three more of Satan's soldiers.

The leader was frantically firing his AR-15 at the Humvee and had to change out clips. As he was reaching for the fresh clip, he saw the silver beast racing toward him, and fumbled the clip and dropped it on the ground. He took cover behind a car, but the car quickly sped off and ran over his foot in the process. It was too late, the menacing grill on the silver beast was almost upon him. He turned and hobbled toward the Grove entrance. The silver beast smacked him from behind and sent him flying into a row of oak trees. He was sprawled in the dust and gravel facedown. He flipped over onto his back and was rocked by excruciating pain in his back and hip. He feebly raised his head and saw the silver beast slowly creeping toward him. He pulled his 9-mil and fired shots at the beast to no avail. On his back and disabled, he cursed at the Humvee. "Who the fuck are you!?" The grill of the silver beast looked like it was grinning at him as it slowly inched up on him and the giant tire rolled onto his left arm and shoulder, crushing them instantly. He shrieked out a blood-curdling scream.

The other militia who had already gathered in the park were now running back toward the entrance having heard the shots fired. They opened fire on the Humvee. The Humvee spun its tires and shot toward the group and ran over and mangled as many as it could before it made a 360 turn and sped out back to the intersection. The Humvee took a sharp right and sped quickly toward the beach, then took a left and disappeared into a neighborhood section. The cars that were still at the intersection and had witnessed the carnage all honked in appreciation as the Humvee steamed out of the Grove and down Sloat Avenue before disappearing. In the distance they could hear sirens coming. Late to the party as usual.

Coffee Talk

"So...you got into a shootout with sex traffickers and the guy who is the prime suspect in our homicide case was the one doing the shooting and he saved your life?" Natalie stared at Hawthorne.

"Yeah, pretty much," Hawthorne solemnly responded.

"You saw him shoot the bad guys?"

"No. They were already shot by the time I got inside."

"How did SFPD not tie you up with paperwork for the rest of your life?"

"I was already out of there by the time they arrived."

"They don't know you are involved?"

"Affirmative."

"Oh boy." Natalie blew out a breath and stared out the window of the small coffee shop they were sitting in. "So where is Hitsman?"

"I don't know. I stopped by his hotel on the way back and he's checked out." Hawthorne tried to steer the conversation away from himself. "So, what was the information that was so urgent that you had to fly out to tell me in person?"

"I found out that Hitsman also went to high school with Clark and Kent."

"Well, that would explain why he was at the reunion. What else?"

"That's it," offered Natalie as she took a sip of her coffee.

"That's it? You flew all this way just to tell me that?"

"Hey, I flew on my dime. Plus, I have a lot of miles that I need to use, and I like San Francisco."

"Oh boy." Hawthorne chuckled. "Ok. We now know that Kent and Clark were involved in sex trafficking. Clark was doing the books and laundering the money. The question is, was Hitsman involved as well and then had a change of heart, or did he find out about them and then decide to take them out?"

"I don't think he was involved," chided Natalie. "His background doesn't show any connections and he has a good standing in his profession. Didn't you also say he was terminal?"

"That's what he said."

Natalie pondered. "So... he has nothing left to lose and he finds out his pals from high school are evil child traffickers, he decides to go full-on vigilante and take them out before he dies. That makes the most sense to me." Natalie, seemingly satisfied with her deduction, bit into a bacon strip. "We need to find out where he's going and if there is anyone else left on his list."

Hawthorne pulled photos out of the manila envelope he had and spread them on the table. After a minute something caught his eye. "This guy. He was chummy with Hitsman in this photo. Take a look." He slid over two 8x10 photos from the reunion in the gym. "The same guy is with Lim in this photo. He looks like he is part of the entourage." Hawthorne pointed to Gilman in the photo. "He might be the next victim."

"What about the big Samoan?" asked Natalie.

"He looks younger, so probably not from the same class. Probably the bodyguard. See the bulge under his coat. He's carrying. I haven't seen him anywhere else. But this guy here, we find him, we find Hitsman."

Natalie looked at the photo. Though the printout of the photo was slightly out of focus, she could still make out the big toothy grin on Gilman.

Yo Ho Ho

Tears were streaming down Gilman's cheeks. He was laughing so hard he was crying. He wiped away the tears but continued laughing uncontrollably, his gut hurting from laughing so hard. He pulled off the street he was on and drove into some old salmon-colored apartments and parked in a parking lot out of sight from main traffic. As his laughter subsided, he grabbed the mirror on the windshield and angled it so that he could see Amy lying on the back seat. Her mouth was gagged but she was still shrieking and crying. It was the sound of her shrieks and the simultaneous crushing of the morons like bugs that had thrilled him to the point of uncontrollable laughter. He had never felt such bliss before. It was exhilarating and yet meditative at the same time. Gilman's dark eyes met Amy's eyes in the mirror.

"I wish you could have seen it, Miss Australia. It was beautiful. All those crushed and mangled fascist maggots and their unpatriotic blood spilling onto the streets. They will think twice about rioting in this city again." Amy sniffled. "I'm glad you were with me, Amy. It's nice that we can share tender moments and make memories together." Amy softly sobbed. "Ah c'mon. Stop the sniveling. Those guys were a bunch of communist shit stains that have no respect for the flag or life. You're not crying for them, are you?" His voice raised on his last line. Amy shook her head no. "Yeah, ok. I guess you didn't know what was happening since you couldn't see out the window."

Gilman whipped the mirror back into position. He sat still for a few minutes just staring at the spider web cracks in the windshield from all the bullet hits. He was glad Kent had been paranoid and sprung for bulletproofing his Humvee. Gilman pulled his sleeve up and checked the time.

"Amy, we got a little time to kill before our meeting with your boyfriend, but first we gotta deep six the beast. I'm gonna find us a new ride. I'll be back."

Just as he was about to get out of the Humvee, Gilman saw an elderly Asian lady walking up from the building and making her way to a car. He reached into the glove compartment. Gilman approached the lady and told her he was going to need her car for a few hours. He then handed her a giant stack of money and said he would make sure the car got back to her. The little Asian lady took the money, smiled, and slightly nodded and bowed. He said a few words in Vietnamese as he took the keys from her and got into the

Hyundai. He wasn't sure if the woman understood him, but he didn't care. He had grown to appreciate their obedience and kindness after years of working with them. Plus, Kent wouldn't be needing the money or the Humvee.

Gilman drove the vehicle over to where the Humvee was parked and opened the back door and pulled Amy out and transferred her to the back seat of the Hyundai. He drove out of the parking lot and back onto the main road, heading toward the freeway. He was in a good mood. It was still early in the day, and so far he had managed to have the distinct pleasure of firing a Mac-10, participating in a mostly peaceful protest, and shared a tender moment with a hot Aussie. Sweet!

****

Hawthorne and Natalie were in the coffee shop parking lot standing by Hawthorne's rental. "I'm going back to the high school to see if anyone recognizes the guy in the photo with Kent and Hitsman."

"I'm going to check into the hotel and clean up," retorted Natalie. "I'll call SFPD afterward and see where they are with their investigation. Depending on how they react when I mention your name, I'll be able to gauge if they have you on video at the scene of this morning's shootings."

"If I get a lead on where Hitsman is I'll let you know, otherwise let's regroup back at the hotel."

****

Tom pushed on the metal door handle and it clicked. Slowly pushing it open, he walked inside. It was dark as he walked into the auditorium. He looked around but didn't see anyone and kept walking toward the stage. Suddenly, a spotlight blinked on and in the middle of the stage was Amy. She was strapped to a chair, bound and gagged. Tom froze. Her face looked puffy from crying, but she didn't seem to be physically hurt from what he could see. Out of the darkness he heard laughter. Then Gilman spoke from the control room over a PA.

"Tommy, Tommy, Tommy. What am I going to do with you?"

"Why don't you come down here and we can talk about it," Tom shouted.

Gilman laughed. "That's very funny, Tommy. But I do want to thank you for killing Kent and Paul. That was you, right, Tommy?"

"You're smarter than I gave you credit for, Darren. I guess by now you've figured out your next," shouted Tom up to the control room.

"I don't think that's going to happen, Tommy. Paul and Kent were dummies." Gilman paused and inhaled. "Why don't you join me? That way I won't have to kill you and Miss Australia," retorted Gilman.

"Let me think about it."

At that moment, Tom pulled the Glock and fired at the control room, blowing out the spotlight. Blackness engulfed the auditorium. Gilman fumbled on the control panel and flipped a couple of switches and finally found the auditorium lights and turned them on. He looked out onto the stage and couldn't believe what he saw. He saw nothing. Just an empty stage. Amy was gone and there was no sign of Tom.

"Bastard!"

Gilman stormed out of the control booth and ran down the stairs toward the stage with gun in hand. He ran up the side stairs, onto the stage, and around on the stage swiveling his head wildly looking for any sign of Amy and Tom.

"That's right. You better hide, because when I find you, I'm going to beat you half to death and then keep you alive so you can watch me kill Amy. You hear me!? You're dead, Tommy!"

From the left side of the stage, he heard music start playing. It was the familiar *Pirates of the Caribbean* theme. Gilman stopped and peered into the darkness, then fired a couple of shots in the general direction of the music. From behind him there was a cracking sound, and he turned just in time to see the front of a giant pirate ship swing across the stage and smash into him, sending him flying to the side of the stage. The giant prop rocked back and forth on the guidewire center stage after smacking Gilman.

Tom walked out from the shadows across the stage past the giant ship and over to where Gilman was sprawled out on the other side of the stage. He stood over the unconscious body then knelt down and took the duct tape out of his duffle bag, tightly binding Gilman's hands and feet. He then headed to the center of the stage and pulled a remote from his pocket and clicked it. Two panels in the floor opened up and suddenly Amy ascended from underneath the stage. He rushed to her and quickly started cutting away the hand ties and leg ties and carefully peeled the tape from around her mouth.

"God I hate that psychopath! How did you do that?"

"I got here a little early. It was a bit of a guess as to what he would do, but it was an educated guess. Are you ok?"

"Yeah, I think so. Is he dead?"

"Not yet."

"This asshole killed over a dozen people this morning."

"What are you talking about?"

"I'll tell you after we kill him." Amy got up and started over toward Gilman.

"Woa, woa. I've got this." Tom grabbed her elbow, stopping her. He looked her in the eye. "If anything had happened to you…I can't take that chance. You have to leave now. I will handle this. And believe me, he will never harm anyone again."

"Can I watch?" Amy asked gleefully.

Tom laughed. "No. You gotta go." He stroked her face and then leaned in and kissed her. "C'mon, you can help get him in the chair, but then you gotta leave."

Amy nodded, disheartened. She really wanted to wrap her hands around his fat neck and squeeze until his sick heart stopped beating. "Will you at least take a picture when you're done?" she asked Tom with a coy smile.

Death By Manilow

As Gilman regained consciousness, he saw Tom sitting in the first row of the auditorium staring up at him. Gilman was tied to a chair that was situated on the auditorium stage. He silently cursed because he had been so close to killing Tom and escaping.

"Welcome back, shithead. You know, I thought the three of you were just high school bullies and dickwads, but it turns out you were much more. Somehow, you idiots were able to run one of the biggest sex trafficking operations in California for over fifteen years. I'm guessing you were the brains behind it, because Kent was too dumb to have been able to pull this off himself."

Gilman sat still, not even trying to break free. He just eyed Tom, looking for a sign of weakness. Tom walked up the stage stairs toward him. Gilman looked down to his left and saw a set of headphones resting next to him. They were hooked up to what looked like a tuner or pre-amp.

"I thought about turning you over to the police, but I can't take the chance that you'll skate on a technicality, and prison is much too good for you anyway. What you did to those girls is unspeakable. So, I've decided to quietly handle this on my own. Well, it's not going to be too quiet for you."

Tom stood in front of Gilman, glaring down at him. Gilman glared back with fiery eyes.

Tom looked around at the stage and the rafters. "This auditorium brings back a lot of memories. Lots of plays and rallies and school activities took place here. One activity stands out more than the rest. The year we had the talent show. You remember that, don't you? You had a significant role."

Both Tom and Gilman flash back to that infamous night.

****

1986 California

Bobby Eberley waited in the wings of the stage while Marilu Pringle finished her cheerleading dance routine. His hands were at his side, but he nervously rolled his fingers in and out, keeping them limber. He felt a bead of sweat trickle down the side of his face, down his neck, and slip past his shirt collar. He was hot and wasn't used to wearing a suit and tie. Bobby was excited but nervous. He had never been on stage in front of so many people. Well, he had never been on stage at all. What if he froze, or worse, played the wrong notes? He was a freshman and small for his age, but he had long fingers which gave him an edge playing piano, which he had been practicing for three years. He wasn't a prodigy, but he was good and had potential.

Parents and students packed the Cabrillo High School auditorium attending the first ever student talent show. Marilu wrapped up her dance routine with a double pirouette while tossing her baton high into the rafters. The baton came close to a bucket that was precariously set on guide wires. She caught the baton and bowed to the applause of the audience.

She skipped off the stage past Bobby as the MC of the talent show walked to the center of the stage and introduced the next act. The stagehands scurried and rolled a piano out to center stage and then retreated into the shadows backstage.

Bobby heard his name called and walked out toward the piano. Each step quickened his heart, which was now pounding like a metronome in his head. He scooted the piano bench back and sat down, then glanced out toward the audience but saw only darkness because of the spotlight in his eyes. He took a deep breath and placed his hand on the keys and played the first distinct chord to Frédéric Chopin's Prelude in C Minor, which had been popularized by Barry Manilow in his hit song "Could it be Magic" just a few years earlier. The chord rang throughout the auditorium and was followed by the next chord and the next as the song built toward its first refrain.

Backstage, one of the stagehands, Tommy Hitsman, watched from the shadows. He was enjoying the performance when he noticed movement behind one of the thick black curtains off to his right. He moved toward the curtains and heard muffled laughter. As he took a peek around the curtain, he saw two boys, one acting as a lookout and the other untying a rope used for the stage props and guide wires. He recognized both boys. Former friends of his. One of the boys glanced over at Tom and sneered. When the rope came loose, the boys snickered and then tugged on it.

There was a loud crash on the stage and the entire audience gasped. Tom ran back around to the side and stopped in his tracks. Bobby Eberly was drenched in a gooey yellow liquid which had crashed down on him and the piano. Remnants of the liquid were still dripping like molasses down from a bucket that had been hanging in the rafters. The audience burst out into horrified laughter. Bobby knocked the piano bench over and wiped his face before running stage left, but slipped and fell, resulting in even more laughter from the audience. Within minutes there were teachers backstage searching for the culprit who had done this horrible deed. Mr. Carbon, the Dean of Men, wrangled the stagehands into a single line. One by one he asked them if they had seen who had pulled the prank. Tom looked out onto the sea of people in the audience and spotted the boys staring at him with a "We are going to kill you if you say anything, you little dipshit" intense glare.

"Did you see who did this?"

Tom's attention snapped back to Mr. Carbon's piercing eyes and then back to the audience.

"Don't look away, answer my question!"

Tom looked back at the intense dark eyes. He could smell alcohol on Mr. Carbon's breath. "No," he said.

Mr. Carbon clenched his jaw and evaluated Tom and the other stagehands. "Listen to me very carefully. If I find out one of you had a hand in this, then you better be wearing steel britches come Monday morning, because I'm going to be doing some ass kicking!"

Fifteen minutes after Mr. Carbon's diatribe, Tommy hurried through the crowd of people spilling out into the parking lot of the school. They were all mortified for the little boy who had, as it turned out, been the recipient of a bucket of melted cheese. Tom quickened his pace as he wanted to get out of there as soon as possible. His Dodge Colt was parked in the east parking lot away from the main parking area because he didn't want to take the chance that someone would bang it up. He had saved up money his freshman year, and although it was not a cool car, it had wheels, and therefore freedom. He had already endured having it vandalized the day after he bought it. He was slipping the key into the driver's side lock when he felt a tremendous blow to his kidney as he was shoved up against his car. Tom turned and saw the two boys who had pulled the prank standing in front of him. They had a malevolent look between them, like two hungry junkyard dogs.

The bigger of the two boy's, the jock, got in Tom's face and said, "I better not find out you ratted us out, Hitsman, or we're going to make it a sport of Hitting Hitsman."

Tommy, still reeling from the kidney punch and working to catch his breath, nodded in understanding.

"You cross us, and you sign your death warrant, you got that?" said the other boy.

They shoved him one more time against the car. Then like clockwork, a new metallic blue Mustang Cobra 2 roared up and skidded to a stop. The two bullies opened the passenger door and jumped in. The driver, wearing a big cheesy grin, flipped him off and peeled out. Tom watched the angry red taillights pull away and dart across the parking lot at mach-two speed. He unlocked his car door and got in his used Dodge Colt. His side felt like it had been hit by a sledgehammer. Gripping his steering wheel as if he was trying to strangle it, Tom looked out onto the dark pavement through teary eyes. He swore one day he would get these bastards back. One day.

****

The day had arrived. Tom got closer to Gilman. They locked eyes.

"I heard that Bobby never played piano again because of your little shit prank. And all because you two idiots thought it was cheesy to play a Barry Manilow song. In case you still haven't figured it out, Bobby was playing a classical piece, you moron."

Gilman's cheek twitched and he looked at Tom quizzically.

"Screw it, I'm wasting my saliva. Well, tonight is payback—or playback, as you'll soon find out." Tom bent down and picked up the headphones and held them up in front of Gilman. "I have here a set of top-of-the-line Sony headphones. They are attached to this tuner, which a friend of mine modified to be able to output up to 200 decibels. Prolonged exposure to 130 decibels will make a man physically sick and leave him with hearing loss. In the range of 150 decibels we are talking about the rupturing of eardrums. It would be like standing right behind a jet during takeoff. Once you get up into the 180 to 200 decibels, you are looking at internal organs rupturing and death. The sound waves alone will kill you, especially if they have nowhere to go but into your ears."

Gilman cursed through the gag in his mouth.

"Tonight, we are going to start the evening off with Chopin's Prelude in C Minor as interpreted by Barry Manilow in his chart-topping hit, "Could it be Magic."

I'm going to start you out at ninety decibels to get you acclimated quickly."

Tom put the headphones on Gilman's head. Gilman tried to shake them off to no avail as they were extremely tight fitting.

Tom plugged his iPod into the tuner and turned it on, turning the dial to ninety. He then navigated to his music and pulled up "Could it be Magic." He hit play.

The opening C chord hit Gilman like a thousand sledgehammers slamming into his head. His body contorted in shock, and he let out a primal grunt. His neck muscles bulged, his eyes bugged out. After about ten seconds, Tom reduced the sound back down to thirty decibels. Gilman could only hear a loud tone. He was sure he was deaf. An animalistic growl escaped from behind his taped mouth, but Gilman couldn't hear it.

"What's that you say, old chap? Louder? Sure thing. I can accommodate that request. Let's try 130 decibels." Tom increased the volume to 130 decibels and showed his screen to Gilman. Gilman's eyes grew wide and he struggled and moaned. "Ok, Barry, take it away! Tom started the song from the top, and with the first strike of the opening chord, Gilman's eyeballs popped out of their sockets and dangled onto his cheeks like two bloody testicles attached by the retina. His body jerked violently then went limp. Blood began to trickle out from his orifices.

Tom stared blankly at Gilman for a few seconds. He looked down at his modified iPod and saw that the LCD screen was flickering. What he thought was 130 decibels was now flickering and showing him that the number was really 180. *Fucking Randy*, he said to himself. He looked back up at Gilman. How disappointing. Yes, he got what he deserved, but it was a bit anticlimactic not having been able to work up to eyeball-popping status slowly. He had really wanted to torture Gilman. Still, if only Bobby could be here to see this. He thought about taking a selfie with him so that he could send it to Bobby someday, but then pushed that impulse out of his head. No need to create incriminating evidence.

Tom moved toward Gilman. He pulled the photo of the young girl he had in his pocket and placed it in Gilman's shirt pocket. "Fuck you, Darren. I'll see you in hell." He looked down at the iPod and at the photo of Barry Manilow. "And as for you, you're worth every Grammy you ever won. Way to go, Manilow." Tom strolled off toward the back of the stage.

"Hold it!"

Tom turned and saw Hawthorne walking down the side aisle of the auditorium toward the stage. He had his gun drawn. Tom sighed, stopped and waited. Hawthorne slowly walked up the side stairs, his gun still aimed at Tom. Hawthorne looked at Gilman strapped in the chair and winced. "Jesus." He got closer to Tom then cautiously lowered his gun. Nodding toward Gilman and pointing his gun at the earphones, he asked, "Metallica?"

Tom shook his head and said, "Manilow."

Hawthorne furrowed his brow and said, "Huh. I never would have guessed. Copacabana?"

"Nah, too obvious. I went with 'Could it be Magic.'"

Hawthorne nodded. "Yeah, that's a good one, too." Hawthorne looked Tom up and down then looked past him into the dark shadows at the back of the stage.

"Where were you going?" asked Hawthorne.

Tom exhaled and shrugged his shoulders. "Exit stage left."

"And then what?" countered Hawthorne

"And then Elvis will have left the building."

Hawthorne smirked at this remark. Then his face clouded over. "You know I gotta take you in, right?"

"Yeah, I figure you do. No grey areas, right?" Hawthorne took a beat to answer then…

"How much time do you have left?"

"They gave me six to eight months, so I'm guessing about another month."

Hawthorne nodded and looked around. "I'm sorry about that, if it's any consolation. You saved a lot of girls and exposed a criminal operation."

Tom gave a slight nod.

Hawthorne looked over at Gilman's dead body then back at Tom. "I have to ask you. Why all the elaborate killings? Why didn't you just go to the police when you discovered what these guys were doing?"

Suddenly the door at the front of the auditorium flung open and Natalie barged in with her gun drawn. "Hawthorne?"

Hawthorne turned toward her. "Yeah, over here."

Natalie made her way to the stage, covering the area around her. Her eyes grew wide as she saw and registered Gilman's unsightly dead body center stage. She looked back over at Hawthorne. "Where's Hitsman?"

Hawthorne responded, "He's…" Hawthorne looked back over his shoulder and all he saw was an empty dark stage and black curtains wavering. A knowing look flickered in his eyes. "He's gone. I missed him."

Natalie climbed the steps onto the stage and holstered her gun. She walked over to Gilman. "Jesus, what the hell?"

Hawthorne cleared his throat. "I guess it's true what they say. Listening to loud music in your headphones will make you go deaf, or in this case, death." Hawthorne winked at Natalie and started back toward the front of the auditorium.

Natalie started after him. "Back in the day, we all looked like that after a Guns N' Roses concert. Loudest concert I ever went to."

"Today, I'm more of a Barry Manilow kinda guy," replied Hawthorne as they stepped out into the bright sun.

Life's a Breeze

Three weeks later, Hawthorne and Natalie were sitting at their respective desks when a package arrived for Natalie. She grabbed the manila envelope from the courier and opened it up with her pocketknife. She pulled out the documents and started going through them. She stared at one of them and a look of concern came over her. She got up from her desk and went over to Hawthorne's desk.

"You're not going to believe this."

"What's up?"

"This just came in. It's a supplement to the medical reports we had on Hitsman. He didn't have cancer."

"What!?" exclaimed Hawthorne.

"It was a misdiagnosis."

"Are you sure?"

"Yeah, it's right here. Apparently, it was a misdiagnosis but they didn't catch it until later. Hitsman was supposed to follow up with an oncologist but he never went. Had he gone they would have caught it and let him know, but since he was a no show it got missed."

"So Hitsman didn't know?"

"Apparently not. No one ever followed up with him. Typical bureaucracy." She handed the document to Hawthorne.

Hawthorne read it intently and then shook his head and smiled. "Never ceases to amaze me."

****

A red jeep pulled up a sandy driveway and parked in front of a beachside bungalow. A man dressed in a Hawaiian shirt and khaki shorts took a sip from a bottle of Arnold Palmer, placed it back in the cup holder, and turned off the engine. He stepped out of the driver's door and went around the front of the jeep to the passenger side door, opened it, and reached in and scooped up a fluffy Maltese dog. He set him down on the pebbly ground and walked up the entryway and opened the front door. He looked back at the dog, who was still sitting next to the jeep.

"C'mon Marty. I got some of those chicken treats you like. Treats, buddy!"

The dog let out a happy yelp and made a tail-chasing circle to his right and then ran up the entryway and into the bungalow. The bamboo door closed behind him. From inside the bungalow, Marty and Tom were greeted by a female with an Aussie accent. After a few minutes, the distinct sound of a needle making contact with a scratchy vinyl record was momentarily heard until the music kicked in and blared out from the old vintage speakers. *Her name was Lola, she was a showgirl. With yellow feathers in her hair and dress cut down to there…*" Barry Manilow's Copacabana rang out into the tropical air and floated up toward the blue sky and echoed off the palm trees, drifting into the wind, where life becomes a breeze.

THE END

Thank you for sticking with me until the end. I hope you had a few laughs and maybe even learned something you didn't already know. If you enjoyed Terminal Hitman I would be grateful if you would let others know by leaving a review.

Thank You.

Sincerely

Jeff Bonilla

ABOUT THE AUTHOR

Jeff Bonilla is a former police officer. He is also an accomplished musician and songwriter, and his music can be found on all digital platforms. He enjoys writing about police officers and criminals and likes to inject music into his writing. He lives in Southern California with his Maltese, Marty. Other books by Jeff Bonilla: *So You Want To Be A Cop*.